P9-DVO-581

SEVEN
CLUES
TO
HOME

SEVEN CLUES TO HOME

Gae Polisner and Nora Raleigh Baskin

ALFRED A. KNOPF · NEW YORK

THIS IS A BORZOI BOOK PUBLISHED BY ALFRED A. KNOPF

This is a work of fiction. Names, characters, places, and incidents either are the product of the authors' imagination or are used fictitiously. Any resemblance to actual persons, living or dead, events, or locales is entirely coincidental.

Text copyright © 2020 by Gae Polisner and Nora Raleigh Baskin
Jacket art copyright © 2020 by Phil Pascuzzo

All rights reserved. Published in the United States by Alfred A. Knopf, an imprint of Random House Children's Books, a division of Penguin Random House LLC, New York.

Knopf, Borzoi Books, and the colophon are registered trademarks of Penguin Random House LLC.

Visit us on the Web! rhcbooks.com

Educators and librarians, for a variety of teaching tools, visit us at RHTeachersLibrarians.com

Library of Congress Cataloging-in-Publication Data is available upon request.
ISBN 978-0-593-11961-7 (trade) — ISBN 978-0-593-11962-4 (lib. bdg.) — ISBN 978-0-593-11963-1 (ebook)

The text of this book is set in 12-point Goudy Old Style.
Interior design by Vikki Sheatsley

Printed in the United States of America
June 2020
10 9 8 7 6 5 4 3 2 1

First Edition

To all the Kings and Queens of Summer Birthdays,
holders of hearts, and readers in search of a story full
of love, friendship, and hope

1

JOY

ONCE UPON A TIME, MY BIRTHDAY WAS FUN.

Emphasis on *once*.

Judging by the sun, I'd guess it's probably not that early. I can hear Isabel and Davy giggling outside my door, waiting for me to wake up. They're more excited about my birthday than I am. I have dreaded my birthday for 364 days, and now it's here.

Yippee.

I'm thirteen.

"Okay, okay," I call out. "You can come in."

It doesn't take but half a second for my bedroom door to fling open and two little bodies to fly through the air and land on my bed.

"Happy birthday, Jolie," Isabel sings. "Davy says happy birthday, too."

My little brother doesn't say much. He's four and a half, and he *should* be talking by now. Mom worries. It's not like I think he has a delay or anything; it's more like he's hiding something. I guess everyone has their secrets.

I know I do.

I still talk to you.

That's my secret.

"I'm still sleeping, you guys," I say. I pull the covers over my head, but I can hear the anticipation in their rapid breathing and the squeaky mouse sounds that Isabel makes when she's happy-nervous. I swear I can even hear Davy tightening his belly muscles in preparation for some major tickling.

And for a moment I forget what day this is. I forget how hard this last year has been. This entire last year I dragged myself up and over whatever it was I had to do. The pain got smaller, but the grief did not.

From under my blankets I start counting, very slowly. It's the slow counting that gets them every time. "One. Two. Three." I can feel two trembling lumps, bony knees and skinny elbows, trying to hold me down.

"Four. Five . . . I hope you don't say the magic word," I call out.

Whatever word comes out of either of their mouths, *that* will be the magic word. All I have to do is wait. And count. They can't help themselves. One of them will say something.

"Six. Seven," I go on.

Isabel tries to clamp her hand over her mouth. I can hear her muffled giggles. We all know *she's* going to be the one to blurt something out. It's always Isabel.

"Eight. Nine."

"Nooo!" she screams.

"That's it!" I yank the covers off my head, and the static electricity makes my hair stick all over my face. I can't see, but I manage to grab hold of my little sister and start tickling her mercilessly.

"That's the magic word," I roar. "The magic word is *no*. And you said it."

Davy tries to slide away. He makes a half-hearted run for the door, but I reach out and capture him, too. Now I've got them both. We are all screams, shouts, and laughing, a tugging, twisting, twelve-limbed octopus creature. Eventually, all the covers slip off the bed like a waterfall, and we end up on the floor in a big pile of arms and legs, and blankets, sheets, and pillows.

And then, just before my mom walks in to see what all the commotion is, with a big smile on her face, and before my older sister, Natalia, steps up behind her and says, "Happy birthday," for a split second, I completely forget what day it is.

I forget that a year ago today is the day after the last day I talked to my best friend, Lukas, for the last time.

And sometimes, in rare happy moments like this one, I can even forget that there, in my desk, in the bottom drawer, is the envelope you left for me, the first clue, on my birthday one year ago today.

 # LUKAS

"YOU'RE NOT GIVING HER THAT, ARE YOU?"

Justin stands at my door, nodding at the small red heart necklace I bought for Joy, which I'm about to slip in its box and wrap in red construction paper. The white envelope, full of six clues, harder this year than any year before, sits on my desk, waiting. Only the first clue will stay in there, get sealed up and slid under her front door. The other five I'll hide in their places around town.

As for the necklace, I'm not sure where I'll leave that. Somewhere near where the last clue leads her back to.

"Well, are you?" Justin moves into the room, stands behind me, mouth-breathing.

"I might," I say, not turning to look at him. "What of it?"

"Nothing. Just wondering."

No, he isn't. "Well, leave me alone, then," I say.

I want him to leave because there's also a note I wrote to her, up on my desk. I'll never hear the end of it if he reads that. But just because Justin thinks he has to act like a jerk

4

to everyone now that he's almost done with high school doesn't mean I have to.

I can tell Joy how I feel, right?

Justin reaches his flip-flopped foot out and touches the pendant with the toe. He knows it's a gift for Joy, even though he doesn't pay too much attention to me or any of the stuff I do anymore, because anyone who knows us knows her birthday is two days before mine. And that we always celebrate them together.

And, yeah, we always do a scavenger hunt, too.

The hunts used to be simple. Just a few easy clues placed all in one area, and some homemade kid present we'd make for one another and stand clutching like a goofy game-show person at the end: a paper-clip bracelet, a rock painted like a polar bear, a Shrinky Dinks key chain, something like that.

But that was before middle school, before I got the dog-walking job and Joy turned eleven and could take that CPR course, which made it so she can babysit the Rogers twins boys for seven dollars an hour, but only on weekend afternoons. So now, for our twelfth birthdays, we agreed to get each other real gifts.

"Just trying to save you the humiliation, bro," Justin says. He leans down to pick up the pendant and turns it by its chain, making me relieved I didn't ask the lady to engrave it.

He tosses it into the air and catches it.

5

I'm not worried about him breaking it or anything. He can be a jerk, but he still takes care of me. It's his job, without Dad around. He will give me plenty of crap, though, so I take care not to turn and let my eyes go to where the note is. If I do that, I'm done for.

He puts the pendant back down on the floor next to me. "It's nice," he says. "But you should trust me on this. Nothing ruins a friendship like declaring your undying love."

"I'm not declaring my love, moron," I say. But my ears burn red and my cheeks set on fire. So what if I am?

"She likes hearts, is all," I add, trying to convince him and me it means nothing. "I saw this at the mall, so I bought it for her. No big deal."

"Right," Justin says. "Forget it. I'm just giving you crap, bro. It's okay. Use your own judgment." He squeezes my shoulder. "You two are tight, so you know her better than I do. Just don't get burned, that's all." I nod, because maybe he really is trying to protect me. "Anyway, I'm heading to Chance's. We're gonna go take the *Angler* out to the Point. Mom won't be home until late, so if I'm not back by dinner, there's stuff in the freezer. Microwave something. She's got a double shift at the Dolphin."

I nod again.

The Dolphin is where Mom works, a diner with a bar in it, so it stays open till midnight on the weekends. The *Angler* is the inflatable fishing boat with the trolling motor that Rand left behind when Mom booted him out last November, once and for all. It's pretty much the only good thing that came from his living here. Everything else was just sad.

Don't get me wrong, though: the *Angler* wasn't a gift or anything; Rand just couldn't fit it on his Harley when he left, and he didn't have his truck anymore because he totaled it, drunk driving. He says he wasn't drunk, but the cop said he was, and that was the last straw. Luckily, no one was hurt, not even him, just the truck and the side of a dumpster on Route 35 and the lamppost that used to be right next to it. Anyway, Mom kicked him out after that, so who needs to think about him now?

"You listening, Lukas? Double at the Dolphin. Late."

I nod again. "Yeah, I heard you."

If you live here long enough, you learn everything in this town is called something Dolphin or Seaside something, even our crappy apartments. The Port Bennington Dolphin Garden Apartments, to be exact, not that dolphins have gardens, so why bother? And not that there's really any garden here, unless you count the small strip of grass with a fence around it, and a few benches and a set of swings that everyone calls a playground. The space that basically separates our building from the train station and tracks.

I'm not complaining. The Port Bennington Dolphin

7

Garden Apartments are fine, if not as nice as our house in the Estates, where we used to live, not that I can remember it so much, but Justin is always saying so.

"Okay," I say, to make sure he knows he's good to leave, since he's still standing there, even as I'm also wondering if he's supposed to be home later, to keep an eye on me. Not that I need him to, but sometimes, when Mom is out late, she likes him to be here with me, even when Rand was still here. If he's not back, I won't rat him out, but it does cross my mind to make him think I might, because then maybe he'd take me with him to the Point. The Point and the lighthouse at Execution Rocks are the two coolest places on earth, even if I haven't actually been out to the lighthouse yet. Who doesn't love a place called Execution Rocks? With or without Justin, I'm going to go one day really soon.

"Have a good time" is all I say.

When I'm sure Justin is gone, I wrap the pendant, carry it to my desk, and reread the note. I decide to add something else, something Justin made me think of. So I rip that one up and start again, writing the whole thing over with new stuff. I reread it, weird nerves squeezing my chest, but the stuff I added makes it better.

When I have it all wrapped and I'm ready to go, I glance back at it all. I'm still not sure but I have a whole day to make up my mind.

2

JOY

I NEVER HAD THE CHANCE TO OPEN LUKAS'S ENVELOPE, THE first clue, which would have led me to the first stop on my Birthday Scavenger Hunt. I never had the chance, and then when I did—days later, after things calmed down, after the police came to our door, after the funeral, after everyone had come and gone, family, friends and strangers, teachers and kids—I didn't want to anymore. I put it away in my desk, and I never looked at it again.

"You're not eating," my mom says. She pushes my bowl of milky, sweet rice cereal, topped with fresh strawberries, closer, but I'm not hungry.

"I will, Mom." I look up across the table and smile. "Thanks."

I've learned to smile, because if I don't, everyone gets all worried. For a while, my mom and dad wanted me to see a therapist, someone aside from the lady doctor who came to our school. But Lukas Brunetti is *my* friend, my *best* friend, and I didn't need my own special doctor to tell me that.

I still can't talk about Lukas in the past tense. I just can't.

I take a big spoonful of my birthday breakfast as Isabel and Davy come clomping down the hall. From the sound of their footsteps, I can tell they are carrying something big. Usually I know what present my family has gotten me before I open it; usually because it's something I asked for or because Isabel can't keep a secret.

But this year I haven't asked for anything, so I have no idea what my little brother and sister are lugging into the kitchen. Whatever it is, my dad is right behind them.

"Surprise!" he calls out.

We are all crowded around our kitchen table, but I am the only one still sitting down. Natalia came running in from the bathroom, her wet hair half up in a towel twisted like a turban, shouting, "Wait, wait for me. Don't start singing yet."

Isabel gives the present one last shove along the floor, and she tells me, "Open it, Jolie." Davy stands next to her, with his arms stiffly at his sides, because he is trying *so* hard not to tear into the wrapping himself. Lukas used to think that was so funny.

Then, even though I don't want my brain to do it, there is a flash of a memory from when we were in school. I am eight years old, and so proud and excited, standing in front of the whole class. I can smell the confection, the sugar, the homemade sweetness, still softly rising into the air.

Now there is something telling me that if I don't remember this, it will all float away. If I don't tell the stories—of cupcakes and scavenger hunts and holes in the sand—they will be lost forever.

I must have that sad, faraway look on my face, because Isabel is stamping her feet, and Davy's baby morning breath is warming the back of my neck, and Natalia is looking at me, with concern, from across the table. My mom puts her hands on my shoulders like she needs to hold me up, and my dad lifts the box and puts it on the table in front of me.

"Happy birthday, my sweetheart," he says.

"What is it?" I slide my fingers under the crinkly paper, and I *am* smiling. I *am* excited. The first bit of writing from the cardboard box underneath appears: ELECTRIC.

"What could it be?" I ask. My hands are moving faster to keep up with my heart beating.

But Isabel can't wait one more second. She dives in, pulls off the last, long sheet of wrapping paper.

"It's a . . ." She stops. "What is it?"

It's a guitar.

It's an electric guitar, and it's real. According to the writing on the box, it comes with its own case, plugs, wires, and a small amplifier. I draw in my breath. "Oh, I love it," I whisper.

"You'll be a real kickass now," Natalia says. Our mom looks, but she doesn't reprimand my sister for her language.

My dad is already cleaning up the wrapping paper.

"You'll have to take lessons," he says. "But now you can play and sing along with yourself."

I want to sing. I do. I used to sing a lot. All the time.

"They told us at the music store that it's actually easier to play an electric guitar," my mom is explaining. "Something about the weight of the strings. But if you want, we can return it and get the other kind. Whatever you want."

I take it out of the box, and it's resting in my hands like it belongs there. It's red and shiny and skinny and totally awesome. Davy reaches up and plucks one of the strings. It makes a muted, whiny sound, not much like music.

"You're a natural, Davy," I tell him. He looks at me and grins. He might not talk a lot, but he's got a great sense of humor.

More presents.

Natalia got me an Ariana Grande easy-chord songbook. We both love Ariana. Isabel hands me a little box of psychedelic guitar picks. And everyone has a handmade birthday card for me, and suddenly it all becomes too much, too much for one person.

It's not that all this *love* is too much for one person—like me—and it's not because I'm too sensitive or I cry too easily; it's because, for some people, life is so unfair.

I heard your story before I even knew who you were.

Once upon a time, a long time ago, there is another kid with a summer birthday, a boy, and he is standing next to me, and I am holding cupcakes. The boy is little as I am, but he already comes with a big story, a story I had heard around the neighborhood, about his family, about him, about his older brother. I heard a story from kids at school, from my own sister, and believe me, it wasn't a good one. I wasn't looking straight at him and he hadn't even *spoken* to me yet, but I already knew the story wasn't true.

LUKAS

"HEY, LUKAS, YOU TOO?" JOY SAID, FOLLOWING ME TO THE front of the room, where Mr. Carter was motioning for us.

"Me too, what?" I asked, even though I should have known, but this was way back in second grade.

"August," she said. "Both of us! See?"

"Oh yeah, right." She was talking about our birthdays.

"What day is yours?" she asked, and when I said mine and it turned out to be only two days after hers, she said, "How weird is that? What are the chances?"

All of this happened on the last day of school, because Mr. Carter, our teacher, had told us he'd use the last day of school for summer birthdays. That way, we'd get the same treats and attention the other kids got. No one even stood up when he called July. Then he called August, and her and me both stood up and headed to the front of the room.

I knew her name well, of course—Joy Fonseca. But even though we'd been in class together a whole year, and even though her family's apartment was in the building right next to ours in Dolphin Gardens, that was the first

14

real thing she ever said to me, the first time it seemed like she wanted to be talking to me on purpose, at least.

Hey, Lukas, you too? . . . What are the chances?

I remember it all perfectly, how she was skinny and small, and had this gigantic Tupperware container filled with homemade cupcakes, vanilla *and* chocolate, all swirled with thick tie-dye frosting, she was trying to maneuver. And I had a shoebox of slice-and-bake cookies I had made with my brother's help, because I hadn't told Mom my birthday was going to be celebrated.

Weird how those few seconds stay in my head. The sugar smell of her cupcakes wafting up, the way she said her words all stiff and formal, which can still sound more like a grown-up's than a kid's.

What are the chances? Both of us in August, she had said, or something like that.

I had answered with math. Or tried to. "Well, twenty-two kids divided by twelve months is . . ." But I couldn't finish the problem that was forming in my head.

"You've got the right idea, Lukas," Mr. Carter had said, stepping up to pat me on the back. "There's definitely a math problem to be solved here."

But not by me, at least not back then. Luckily, Joy didn't care. She just laughed, getting what I was trying to do.

I still got embarrassed, and my words trailed off, and my face went hot, and my hands got all gross and clammy.

"You good at math, Lukas?" Joy had said, but it was more

like she was telling me than asking. Then she had reached a hand up to flip her thick brown hair off her face and nearly dropped her container, with all the pretty rainbow cupcakes about to spill out. I quickly hoisted my shoebox under my arm so I could help her. "But it must be less than that, right?" she added once we'd secured things. "Because we're *both* in August, so that makes it out of eleven months, not twelve."

She had giggled, unsure of herself, but we knew right then that we both liked math pretty good, which is part of what got us hanging out together. For the rest of that whole summer, and after that. Math and word puzzles and riddles and scavenger hunts and playing outside the Dolphin Garden Apartments on the strip of grass with the swings. Even in the years that came after, when we didn't actually wind up in classes together.

That day, in Mr. Carter's class, was the day that sealed it. I had put my shoebox down and took her big plastic container for her, holding it while we walked the rows of desks together, her doling out those tie-dye-swirl cupcakes.

Afterward, she'd said, "Thanks, Lukas, you're nice," her voice rising on those last two words, almost like she was surprised or asking a question.

Like it took her a whole school year to realize it.

Later she explained how everyone talked about us— Mom and Justin and me—because my dad was dead and my mom worked so much, and so Justin and me were alone a lot of the time, off in the playground or skateboarding down Main Street, and younger than other kids whose parents might let them hang out alone. Except I wasn't alone, because Justin was always watching me. But probably from the corner or something sometimes, so he could talk to his friends and I didn't have to feel like such a baby anymore.

"Not to be mean or gossipy or anything," Joy had cleared up. "More like because people worry about you and your brother . . . because you have no dad and all."

And, anyway, by the end of third grade, Mom was dating Rand, and he was great at first, so it was almost like we had a dad, so maybe people wouldn't talk about us anymore. But then he moved in and started to show his true drinking colors and so everyone pretty much knew—or, worse, heard because of their fighting. So, yeah, he could be a jerk, but he could also be good and helpful and fun, so it was harder than you'd think to get rid of him.

"But you're nice, not wild . . . not a troublemaker," Joy had said to me that first summer, a few weeks after school ended, and we were hanging out a lot together.

"What if I'm both?" I asked, probably wanting to sound tougher than I was.

She kicked a pebble in my direction. "Then I like you even better," she had said.

I smile, thinking about that now as I lock our front door and step outside into the bright sunshine.

The good thing about not being rich anymore is you live closer to town, practically right on the edge of it. I head across the grass, past the swings, around the corner, and toward Main Street, picking up my pace toward Vincent's.

3

JOY

I DON'T KNOW WHAT IN THE WORLD TELLS ME THIS IS A GOOD idea, but it's too late now. It's done. I did it. I opened the envelope. And now I'm going to read it.

Here goes.

It's okay. I'm not going to do anything. I'm just going to read it.

> It's not about money
> But it is about dough.
> In a world with no dolphins,
> Surely, you'll know.
>
> P.S. Starting easy. Basically a "gimme."
> You're welcome. ☺
>
> Find the table with the other kind of Pie.

There. I read it.

I stare down at his handwriting, which I'd know any-where, and, yeah, it hurts. It's like someone has a clamp and it's pressing down on my ribs, squeezing my heart, but I can still breathe, which is a good sign.

I am whelmed. But not overwhelmed.

And, yes, that's a word, thank you very much.

At first, and for a long time, whenever I thought about that day, about what happened, I'd be crying so hard, my lungs tightened and no air could get in. It was once so bad, my dad had to rush me to the emergency room. The closer we got to the hospital, the more and more I thought I was going to die.

They told us, at the hospital, it was a panic attack.

So now I know.

And now I can breathe.

So I look down at the clue again.

Basically a "gimme." You're welcome. ☺

You're right. Thank you. This is an easy one.

Vincent's Pizza.

It's where we eat sometimes, on weekends or after school. I haven't stepped foot in there, not once. Since. But I know exactly where Lukas means, and not just the restaurant, but which exact booth. I bet it's the one by the window that looks out to the landing, and for a tiny second I think I can taste on my tongue sweet pineapples doused in white sauce.

The worst, I know. I know!

Of course, I was making money babysitting before Lukas got that job walking dogs. But eventually he was making more money than I was watching people's kids, their *human* kids. You'd be surprised how many people around here will pay someone just to take their dog for a walk and pick up the poop in a plastic bag. But, at first, I had all the money. I made twenty-one dollars in one Saturday afternoon, and the first place we went was Vincent's Pizza.

Third booth on the right.

"Jolie, you okay in there?" It's my mom, outside my bedroom door.

I guess they worried when it got quiet, when I stopped picking out notes on the guitar. There was a long time they made me keep my door open whenever I was alone in my room. I sure don't want that to happen again.

"I'm fine, Mommy."

I slip Lukas's note back into the envelope, hide it under my pillow, and pick up the guitar again. It's actually not that hard. There is a diagram in the book Natalia got me that shows you where to put your fingers. I've already learned two chords. I try to open my mouth and sing the words, but I can't. I hold on to the neck, press down on the strings, and, with my other hand, strum, up and down, across the guitar.

"Just practicing," I call out.

I move my fingers around and try another chord, but I keep looking down at the pillow. I can't help but wonder, and soon as I wonder, then wonder turns into a wish, and a wish quickly becomes anxiety.

What if his clue is still there?

Waiting for me.

It couldn't be. And even if that one is there, there's no guarantee that any of the others would still be where he put them. A year later? No way. Reading the clue was one thing, but what I'm thinking now is a bad idea.

Should I go find the second one?

My parents would never let me go look. That, I know for sure. Even if it didn't require heading from place to place, not knowing where I was going or how I was going to get there, my parents aren't exactly loosey-goosey when it comes to letting me wander around by myself.

Besides, all the clues can't still be there.

Can they?

My breathing feels tight.

But then again, what if they are? What if the clues are just waiting out there in the world?

What if I *can* find them?

I bet Lukas was really clever about where he hid the clues. He is smart, really smart. Smarter than anyone I know. Than anyone gives him credit for. Except me.

And I know it sounds stupid, but I always kind of dreamed he and I would get married one day, which probably explains some of the things that came flying out of my mouth, which I am already starting to forget.

Cupcakes and scavenger hunts and holes in the sand.

It can't hurt to look.

I owe him that much.

I shut the Ariana Grande easy-chord songbook, lean my new red birthday guitar carefully against my bed, grab my wallet, and stuff Lukas's first clue deep into the back pocket of my jeans, because whelmed is decidedly better than overwhelmed.

LUKAS

IT'S HARD TO WALK THROUGH THE JINGLE-JANGLING DOOR of Vincent's Pizza with no money, because it smells so good and I haven't eaten yet today, so I'm starving. But I spent my savings on Joy's gift, so I'm going to have to suck it up for now.

So many thoughts hit me with the good smells, and all of them make me happy. Like the time in fifth grade Joy bet me five dollars I couldn't eat a large pizza with pepperoni and onions all by myself, and I had to prove I could, so we stayed there for a whole three hours while I finished.

"Bet your stomach is hurting pretty bad," she said when we were walking home.

"Is not," I insisted. Then we both got quiet, and she started laughing because I was practically running, I had to get home to the bathroom so bad.

Or the other time we decided to order slices with all the gross things on them we never usually eat, like mushrooms and pineapple and Alfredo sauce. We each got to pick the other person's toppings, and Jairo was willing to make it, so I ended up with artichokes, which are gross enough, but pineapple with Alfredo sauce is more disgusting. Joy laughed so hard trying to eat that, the pineapple-flavored white sauce came shooting out her nose.

But mostly what hits me right now is how hungry I am.

Jairo is working today, so I could ask him to spot me a slice, and he would. He's Justin's friend Neco's older brother, and he's, like, twenty already, and way more responsible than Neco. Pretty much the nicest guy in the world. He's worked at Vincent's since high school, so now he's a manager and could do it, but since I'm about to "deface the property," like the sign over the garbage pail says not to do, it doesn't feel right accepting a slice of pizza for free.

It's lunchtime, so at least the place is busy enough to take the attention off me, but not so busy that I can't get the table I wanted by myself, which is also good luck. I head toward it, *our* table, the one we sit at most, whenever it's free. The one where I ate the whole pizza and she ate the pineapple and Alfredo. That's the exact table I need.

I slide into the side facing out to the water and open the newspaper someone left here. I pretend I'm reading and waiting for food.

I turn pages importantly, then twist to see the counter. Jairo is back there, yelling orders. He doesn't see me, and there are, like, seven people lined up, so I slip my pocket-knife out, the one Dad bought Justin when he was in fifth grade, and then Justin gave me for Christmas last year,

25

because now he has a new one, a deluxe, with twelve different things on it, including pliers, a screwdriver, and a bottle opener.

I look up out at the water in the distance, my brain thinking about the best way to carve the clue. But then I wonder about Justin and Chance, and if they're already out on the *Angler*. And suddenly I'm thinking about Rand and the first time he took us out, right after he moved in with us.

✳

Crack of dawn, Saturday, Rand, Justin, and me pile into Rand's truck. We have a cooler full of sandwiches and fresh-baked cookies with us, because last night Mom was making a whole big deal about it, like we weren't just heading to the Point. Now, since there's no back seat for us kids, she stands at the truck window saying goodbye all anxious and stuff, making Rand promise to drive careful and slow and to please not drink any beer.

Just as we're about to pull out, we notice how the sun is coming up, slashing the deep blue horizon with pink, and lavender, and gold. So Mom puts her hand on Rand's on the wheel, and he turns off the engine, and we all get out and sit on the hood, because it's way too pretty not to watch. "Like God himself is painting it," Mom whispers, holding tight to Rand's hand, but I wonder if she's thinking about Dad.

Later, on the *Angler* in the middle of the bay, we choose our sandwiches and sodas, and we're eating and talking and having fun. And then Rand has a beer in his hand, I don't even know where from. And he's drinking it, so him and Justin are fighting, then Justin and me are fighting, because Justin says he's gonna tell Mom, and I'm saying, "Let's don't tell her, because she has enough problems without having to deal with that."

✳

Right on this table, there's stuff carved everywhere, so I don't feel too bad, even if there is a NO DEFACING sign. Dumb stuff and funny stuff and rude stuff, and lots of names and initials carved inside of hearts.

I trace my finger along one of those, mad that my brain is thinking about doing that instead—carving L.B. + J.F. inside some dopey heart just to see what it might look like there, all permanent like that. But what if she saw it? So I'd have to just scratch it right away. Besides, I have to get this clue done, so I pull the newspaper over my hand and dig in. The wood of the table gives easily under the blade, but the curves of the 3 are still hard to get smooth so small, and with my face bent over what I'm doing, I nearly nick myself in the nose, trying.

"How you doing, Lukas?"

I have a heart attack, drop the knife on the table, and flatten my palm. The newspaper drifts and settles over my hand. Jairo stands over me. "You here alone, kid? Eating anything?" He puts a container of red pepper flakes down on my table. A lemony-smelling rag is squeezed in his other hand.

"No, just waiting," I stammer, then add some more information because I don't like to lie, so I need to prop it up with a little truth. "It's Joy's birthday tomorrow. . . . And we do this thing. Like a treasure hunt, kind of. I know that sounds dumb. But I came here to hide one of the clues." Leaving the knife under the newspaper, I slide my hand out, reach in my pocket, and hold out the folded next clue to him. "I was going to tape this here, under the table, if it's okay? It'll be gone by tomorrow, promise. She'll know to come in here and find it."

He unfolds the paper, leaving the black *2* in my chicken scrawl staring down at me like the mark of Zorro.

"'Half up half down what's old,'" he reads aloud, with no breaks or pauses where he needs to, which messes with the rhythm and the rhyme scheme, making my words, the whole clue, sound really stupid. "'Is now new. Ask for her by name, eight-four-three-two.'" He hands the paper back to me. "I don't get it."

"Yeah," I say, my ears reddening. "You didn't exactly read it right. But she will."

"Suit yourself," Jairo says. "So, you want a slice?"

I nod, feeling bad. "Sure, I would. But I don't have any money today."

"Ah, gotcha. No worries. It's on me. Just pay it forward," he says.

When he goes back to put my slice in the oven, I pull the small roll of tape from my pocket and seal the clue under the table, then finish carving the rest of the numbers in:

Find the table with the other kind of PIe.

Pi—3.14.

There.

No way Joy will miss them.

Still, I gouge the oval around them deeper, just to be sure.

4

JOY

THE AIR CONDITIONER SOUNDS EXACTLY THE SAME AS I remember, and I don't know if I ever noticed it before, but now I do. It hisses and spits. It rattles, or maybe that's my heart pounding. In either case, I am afraid to open my eyes as I push open the door and walk into Vincent's Pizza. Instead, I squeeze them shut and I take a long second to wish as hard as I can that Lukas's clue is still here, somewhere. And that I'll be able to find it.

As if wishing a thing can make it come true.

Yeah, yeah, Lukas, I know you think it can't.

Still, I'm only wishing for something small.

I am wishing that no one is sitting at our booth. I wish no one is sitting at our booth. I wish. No one. Is sitting. At our booth.

I open my eyes.

Presto, magic.

No one is.

Getting out of the house had been easier than I expected, but mostly because when Davy was jumping off the arm of the couch, his cape got caught under his foot and he hit his cheek on the coffee table. It wasn't that big a deal. It sure wasn't out of the ordinary, but it did divert everyone's attention long enough for me to announce that Mrs. Rogers, the lady I babysit for, wanted me to stop by to give me a birthday gift, which wasn't a lie because it was true. It's just that it had happened last week.

Natalia looked up from her computer long enough to give me a deadpan look that I couldn't exactly read, but I knew she wouldn't say anything because that's kind of our sister bond.

My dad was holding a bag of frozen peas and trying to get Davy to stay still while he pressed it to his face. Isabel was standing on the arm of the couch, re-enacting exactly what had occurred, while Mom was telling her to stop.

They both looked up and waved at me, and I was out the door.

I slide into our booth, third one on the right, and I tell myself to pretend that this is just any other day. That I'm not here to find a clue that may, or may not, have been left here for me 366 days ago. If I don't worry and get anxious, maybe I'll remember something; if I just open my brain and let it come, maybe it will come to me. My dad always says a watched pot doesn't boil.

Yeah, yeah, I know a pot will still boil even if you are watching it. Very funny.

Outside the window is the too-blue sky, and gulls

31

swooping past. If I changed places and sat on the opposite side, I'd be able to see the seawall and the Sound. But this is my side, my seat. The one I always sat in, while Lukas sits across from me, pizza goo stuck on his face. Tomato sauce on his shirt.

I know, right?

Always tomato sauce on your shirt.

But none of that matters right now; right now I have to take my time and try to sort things out, prepare myself that the clue isn't here. Or prepare myself that it might be.

No one is going to bother me. It's not that kind of restaurant. I can sit here and think. If you want to order, you have to walk up to the counter.

"Can I help you?"

I look up. "Huh?"

I guess it's a waitress because she's wearing a uniform and holding a pad of paper, a pen poised in her fingers. "Can I get you anything, sweetie?" I must be looking at her funny because she adds, "To eat?"

A waitress? That's new.

So I look around—I mean, *really* look around. I see that the big mural on the wall of the Roman Colosseum is different, mainly because there never was one there before. And there is a red-and-white-striped half-umbrella thingy that stretches out over the place where you used to stand and order, and there are waitresses now, too, I guess.

So many things are different. Is anything the same?

Maybe this isn't the right table after all.

But I'm sure he meant Vincent's Pizza, right?

No, it's right. And I'm sure he meant pi.

As in 3.14, Archimedes's constant, the ratio of a circle's circumference to its diameter.

Or did the clue have to do with the time, like 3:14 in the afternoon, and pi was a red herring that was supposed to throw me off?

Hey, what time is it? Shoot, I forgot my cell phone, and I'm starting to panic a little. What if I never figure this out?

And now I'm not breathing so well, either.

"Sweetheart? Do you want anything to eat?" The waitress is still standing here.

I am having one of those weird out-of-body experiences, like I've lost track of my own body and maybe I'm in the wrong moment or the wrong place. Everything gets blurry and freezes. I know what I'm supposed to do: Count my inhale. Count my exhale. Make them longer.

I place both my hands down on the table to calm myself.

The *table*.

I'm sure it's the right one, but *something* is different. The surface is smooth and feels polished—I don't remember that. I lean closer.

It even smells faintly of shellac.

Of course, it's different. It's been a year.

Yes, I know. I'm using my brain. I'm trying, Lukas, I really am.

What could have changed in a year? What could be the same? Where could he have hidden the first clue? I look around.

The basic structure of the room is the same. The layout. The open wood fireplace. The windows and doors and booths. It looks like it's just been redecorated: the painting on the wall. Maybe it's even the same owners and they just wanted a little lift. Spruce the place up a bit. Add a striped awning, and a waitress or two.

"Are you waiting for someone?"

Oh right. She's still here.

Now I feel something new. Anger. Angry at this waitress who won't leave me alone when I'm trying to concentrate.

Angry.

And then at Lukas.

I'm mad at you. You really need to ask why?

For leaving me here. For not being here to explain things. We were supposed to help each other when the clues got too hard. We always did this together. That was the whole fun of it, watching the other person running around, trying to figure it out. Enjoying the hide-and-seek of it.

When we were little kids, we did the whole hunt in one place, of course, like the library or the Dolphin apartments, which was good that one year it rained all day. The wind blew the waves against the seawall, crashing so loud we could hear them. But we were warm and safe inside. I put one clue in that old, dried-out wreath that Mrs. Clemson never took down from her front door. When Lukas reached up to find it, the whole thing disintegrated and crumbled into pieces of dried twigs and gray, papery leaves.

We could hear Mrs. Clemson's shoes clicking on her wood floor inside her apartment, coming closer, so, of course, we ran.

Now, where is your clue, Lukas? Where did you leave it?

I'm so mad at you.

For leaving me here to notice all these changes and not have anyone to talk about them with. I can imagine Lukas's voice, the funny things he'd have to say about that butt-ugly mural.

"No," I snap back at the waitress.

I don't mean to. It just comes out that way.

"Well, you can't sit here." She's not smiling anymore. "It's almost lunch hour. You can't take up a whole booth."

I'm not sure if I'm still angry or sad or just dizzy, but I know I want to hide under my covers, except I'm still sitting here in this restaurant, with a grown-lady waitress looming over me. I want to curl in a ball, which I kind of try to do, but my knees knock into the underside of the table.

Wait, what?

No way.

But maybe.

Maybe?

There's something stuck under here, and it's not gum.

"I'm really sorry," I say quickly.

35

I need to buy more time.

I *am* sorry for being rude, but mostly I don't want to jinx the chances that someone might have been kind enough to leave Lukas's first clue right here. Right where he left it. Right where I am sitting. I feel around with my hand.

"What are you doing?"

I probably look pretty strange right now, bent over and twisting around, trying to look like I'm not doing either of those things. Then my fingers land on what feels like a piece of paper, taped under the table. And I don't want to let go. I want her to go away so I can get under the table and get a good look at what this is before I tug at it.

"I feel like I might be getting sick. Can I get a glass of water, maybe?" I grimace a little, for added effect.

"Okay, but after that, you have to order something or you'll have to leave. Okay?"

My face is about two inches from the table, but I manage to nod. As soon as she's gone, I slip down, ever so slowly, loosen the ends of the tape, and peel it back. I can feel little bits of fake wood coming off, too, but as quickly as I can, I unstick the paper, pull my hand out from under the table, and bolt for the door.

# LUKAS

I'M SWEATING, WALKING UP THE HILL FROM VINCENT'S toward Angel's Consignments, which is Thea's shop, and suddenly remembering the night, last November, when Joy met me outside our buildings because I asked her to, because I needed to talk to her, because I was happy and sad about Rand leaving, and also because it was the Taurid meteor shower, so we were killing two birds with one stone. Maybe I'm thinking about that now because last time I walked past Thea's, she had all those sparkling star lights hanging down in the window, like shooting stars.

✳

"Fifty-fifty is the real answer," Joy says excitedly. "I can't believe I almost forgot to tell you, Lukas. And it even has a name. It's called the birthday paradox."

It's chilly out, and pitch-dark, and Joy and me are lying side by side in an unzipped sleeping bag I brought down to keep us warm. We're allowed to lie like this to watch the meteor shower, so long as we stay here, where her parents can see us from their window. The last one we watched together was the Perseids in August, but it was overcast, so we didn't see much. But this night is crystal clear, and we can actually see the meteors zipping and arcing like magic lasers across the sky.

"I can't believe I forgot to tell you," she says. "It's a real thing. The birthday paradox. That first thing we were ever trying to figure out—in Mr. Carter's class, remember?"

Of course I remember, the day with the cupcakes. But I don't say that because maybe I don't need her to know how I think about it so much. Not that I used to worry about stuff like that, but now it feels too weird, especially with us lying here close together, side by side.

Joy gets impatient, waiting for me to say something, though. She kicks her foot against mine. "Hey, Lukas," she says, "you're not even listening."

She's right and wrong. I am listening, obviously, but not completely. Not like I usually can. Because my mind is a little crazy tonight, probably because of the Rand stuff and, also, the super-bright white streak that's zooming in an arc across the sky, which I'm pretty sure may be an actual fireball.

Where we are lying is on the slanted dirt mound near the swings. In spring, they plant a whole bunch of tall purple-and-yellow flowers with orange tongues that stick out here, because it's right where the sign staked into the ground says DOLPHIN GARDEN APARTMENTS. But this time of year, it's just dirt, and a slope that makes for a good stargazing position.

"Yes, I am," I say. "The birthday paradox. I am, too, listening, Joy."

"Okay, fine," she answers. "So, it's an actual famous paradox about sharing birthdays, of all things. Can you believe it? How did we not ever know that? Mrs. Roessing just told us all about it today."

"What's a paradox?" I ask, adding, "I forget what that is," as if I knew just a few days ago.

"Oh, like a thing that sounds logically impossible, but then ends up being possible. Sort of, kind of," she says. "Mrs. Roessing explained it a whole lot better than I can. Aren't you doing logic problems in Spear's class?"

Mrs. Roessing is her math teacher. Now that we're in middle school, we have homeroom and a few other classes together, but math and social studies, we have different teachers. I have Spear, who kind of sucks, and she has Roessing, who is totally awesome. So, lots of days, we have to share the things the other person didn't get to hear about during the day.

"So, how it goes," she continues, "is that, in a room full of twenty-two people, there's actually a fifty-fifty chance that two of the kids will share the same exact birthday. Fifty-fifty! And in a room of seventy-five people, those chances go up to ninety-nine percent. Remember how we thought it was really, really slim? Like twenty-three divided

39

by twelve divided by something else, or something like that? Anyway, I'm not sure I understand it. I really needed you there to help. Actually, now that I'm trying to explain it, it doesn't make too much sense at all."

I nod, working to focus on the math stuff while also keeping my eye on the sky.

"It's got to be a probability thing," I say, to come up with some sort of answer. "Like the marbles worksheets Ms. Spear had us doing last week in groups. Did you do those?" I ask her. "Those marbles problems?" She shakes her head. "Okay, well, at first they were easy, but then they got more and more complicated. Like: 'If you have a bag with twelve marbles, and seven are purple and three are red and two are green, then what is the probability you reach in and pull out a blue marble?' And the answer is zero, obviously, and the probability that you reach in and pull out a purple marble gets higher, and so on. But there are ways to figure out more specific percentages, too. So, with your birthday paradox . . ." I'm trying to compare that to the marbles problems, but even as I'm saying it, it's all turning to mush in my brain. "Okay, so, like, if there are twenty-three people, you're comparing the first person to twenty-two other people, but then, when you're comparing the next person, she's already been compared to the first person as one of the other twenty-two, so that leaves only twenty-one comparisons, and so on. So your chances actually go up. Right?"

Joy shudders like I've confused her, but then it occurs to me she's cold, so I pull the sleeping bag up around us tighter, feeling instantly weird about it, and even weirder when she squishes right close next to me. So, now my heart is beating fast like someone wound it up too tight, with her this close to me, because ever since we got to middle school, I've been noticing more and more girl things about her. Even when I try my hardest not to.

And I do. I try hard not to.

I never used to pay attention to those things. The girl things. Like, zero attention. Like, not even one tiny bit at all to how her eyes are really dark and serious most of the time, but when she's happy, they start to smile even before her mouth does. Or how some of her clothes fit tighter in spots in a nice way, more than they used to. Or how her hair smells like vanilla most days, but also like firewood in the winter, and cherries in the spring, like the seasons are exploding up out of her.

"Wait, but wouldn't that make the chances less?" she asks, touching one of my fingers with one of hers, maybe accidentally, but still it makes it harder to answer, because now my thoughts are spinning off in that wrong direction even more.

I think her mom notices the girl stuff about her, too, because she doesn't want me in Joy's room so much anymore, and she used to not mind it at all.

"I swear, Lukas," she says, managing to bend her arm up

41

to jab me with her elbow in my side, "sometimes I think an actual alien abducts your brain and only leaves your body here, pretending to care about things."

"I care," I say fast. Probably too fast. "I mean, I'm the one who said we should come out and watch the stars, right?"

"But I'm talking about this birthday paradox thing."

"And I'm trying to explain it, I swear."

She rolls toward me and gives me bug eyes and starts in again, but this much closer, I can smell the sugar-and-fire smell of her hair, so strong it makes it hard to breathe. I make a noise, which she luckily thinks is about the meteors, because she turns away to look up just as another bright light streaks across the sky.

"Quick, make a wish," she says.

"I don't have any."

"Yes, you do."

Joy loves to make wishes, but she knows I think they're kind of stupid. Too much pressure, and, anyway, it's not like they ever come true. Besides, when your dad dies when you're five, it's like everyone is watching and waiting for your wishes, with these super-sad faces, every time you find a penny or blow your birthday candles out. Because they all think they know what you're wishing for, which is for your father to come back, because why would you wish for a new bicycle or Lego set or a new *Pokémon* game when you could be wishing for that? Except the weird thing is, you're not always. I wasn't. Not only because I barely remember him, but also because it would be a dumb, old waste of a wish. I don't care how magical wishes are supposed to be, you can't make a dead man come back again.

So, why wish for something that can't happen? And if you don't wish for that, you end up wishing for something greedy or selfish, like that new bike or a bigger fishing boat, or at least I would, when instead I should wish for Mom to win the lottery or to have a boyfriend again, but one who is way better than Rand.

"So, did you wish for something, Lukas?" She makes an arc in the air with her finger, tracing the trail of the star.

I wish I could kiss you.

"No," I say fast, and she drops her hand, and the air stays silent, with her probably being sad about my answer.

"Lukas?"

"Yeah?"

She finds my fingers with her fingers again, but this time I know it's on purpose, because she squeezes them, which isn't exactly helping my brain from feeling like it may be on actual fire. And so then I'm really thinking about maybe kissing her, but something else happens. For some dumb reason, tears almost come into my eyes. I squeeze them away, feeling super glad it's dark and she can't look over and see me too well.

"I'm sorry," she says. "I know you don't have wishes. I just want you to, Lukas. That's all. Because you deserve them." I nod, working to keep any full tears from escaping, which I'm usually pretty good at, but also I'm not feeling as tough as normal tonight, probably because of everything with Rand and Mom. "But until you do, do you want me to tell you mine?"

I nod again. "Yeah, I would," I say.

"Okay." She lets go of my hand and sits up, making me sit up, too, and the sleeping bag falls down from our shoulders. She bends her knees up and wraps her arms around them and stares again into the sparkling sky. "So, no making fun of me, because I know it sounds corny, but it's also mathematically possible, like, probability-wise, so under your rules, it isn't a waste of a wish."

"Okay, tell me, then."

"It's simple," she says. "One perfect wish that could easily come true."

I sit beside her, listening to her breathe and watching the stars, which seem to be moving around in some weird way, all together and too fast, spinning and winking and changing places like the whole sky has gone crazy and its job is to actually make me feel dizzy, but maybe I've just been staring at them for too long.

"Here it goes, then. I wish we could always be friends."

For a second, everything stops and is quiet in the best way, and I feel steady again, like we're just here, both of us part of the dirt and the earth and the ground. Then a dog barks, and someone yells for someone else from a window, and a train whistle blows, sharp and loud, and blows again, and it's a long, sad sound at night, in the dark, like this. Way sadder than in daytime, so it sits like a rock in my chest, because it reminds me of all the people in the whole wide world who are still waiting for someone to come home.

5

JOY

I BLINK IN THE BRIGHT SUNLIGHT ON THE SIDEWALK OUTSIDE of Vincent's Pizza, trying to figure out if I am dreaming or not. Am I really holding Lukas's second clue in my hands?

I'm not mad anymore, not at anyone. In fact, I feel something I haven't felt in a long time.

I think I'm giddy.

But now the problem is, I have no idea what the clue means.

> Half up, half down,
> What's old is now new.
> Ask for her by name,
> 8-4-3-2.

I look up and down the street—there are barrel planters every few feet, overflowing with purple, red, and yellow blossoms, and more flowers in baskets hanging from the streetlamps—and then I look up into the sky.

46

Well?

I wait for you to say something, but all I see is the sun, pretty much directly above, so it must be close to noon. I figure it's been over an hour since I left, and if Davy stopped crying and Isabel stopped jumping, my parents will start turning their thoughts to me again.

I should have grabbed my phone. At least I could check in, maybe buy myself a little more time. Lukas and I never left our clues that far apart. So if the third clue is still there, it's got to be around here somewhere.

If I could just figure out what *half up, half down* means.

Port Bennington isn't rich or fancy or anything, but it's not as small a town as you might think. There are five elementary schools, two middle schools, and one huge high school. Tourists come only to this part, though, the pretty part with the nice sidewalks and flower boxes, but in the summer there's sure a lot of touristy activity, filled with lots of people who like boats and water.

You know I never liked the water the way you do.

The people here are in no rush to go anywhere fast, eating ice cream, holding two, three, four designer shopping bags, wearing dressy shorts and high-heel sandals and T-shirts printed with really creative slogans like PORT BEN-NINGTON.

I know, right?

And if you couldn't tell the tourists by what they are wearing, Lukas always says, you can tell who the out-of-

47

towners are by how rude and inconsiderate they are, how they walk down the sidewalk, chatting, licking their cones, pointing at things in the window displays, three and four across, so no one else can get by. Like those three, up there by the green truck.

They are walking so obnoxiously slow, too.

But, anyway, everyone has to slow down when they get about midway up the street, because good old historic Main Street is basically on a twenty-five-degree angle. And about halfway up, it starts to feel like you are climbing a mountain, which is exactly how I feel right now.

I step off to the side and try to stand in the shade, but there's not much and it's boiling hot out. I don't even have a hat or sunglasses. I'm probably getting a sunburn, and my mother will be mad. Lukas would always be brown by this time of year, and he never wore sunscreen.

Never wears. Never wore.

Knowing his handwritten note is in my back pocket lets me imagine him, but just for the tiniest fraction of a second. Then I rub it away and concentrate on all the people busy with whatever people who are not busy tend to do.

Outside of Grayson's Florists, a lady in a yellow smock is watering the planters.

A little farther down, a mother is begging her toddler to stop whining and get up off the sidewalk.

There is a family of four, about halfway up the block, trudging toward the fudge shop, and none of them look like they need any fudge.

About halfway up.

And halfway down.

Oh my God. Oh my God. That's it.

I did it.

That's what you meant, isn't it?

Lukas wanted me to walk out of Vincent's and to stay on Main Street. To head this way. *Up* from the pizza shop. But it's not enough.

What did he mean by *half up?*

Halfway to what? Halfway to where?

You need a beginning and an ending point to know where the middle is.

I don't know where, but I start walking, anyway. In fact, I start running, which, in this heat, is not such a good idea. I run all the way to the top of the block. Then all the way down, I start back up again. Up. Straight up.

Nobody turns to look at me, or wonder why this just-turned-thirteen-year-old kid is running up and down Main Street like she's cross-training for the Ironman. Or just lost her mind.

My shirt is drenched. Finally I stop, lean against a cool brick wall of the Port Bennington Savings and Loan, and take the clue out of my back pocket.

I unfold it like it's made of glass.

> Half up, half down,
> What's old is now new.
> Ask for her by name,
> 8-4-3-2.

But this whole town is old, Lukas.

That's not going to help. And who is *her?*

No, if anything is going to help, it's going to be the numbers, of course. Lukas would know that I'd understand numbers. But I don't.

Eight thousand four hundred thirty-two?

There must be numbers around here somewhere. Addresses?

The fudge shop—where I see the family of four inside, cooling off in the air-conditioning—is at 119 Main Street. The dry cleaner's across the street is number 120. Even on one side, odd on the other. But not anything anywhere close to eight thousand.

> 8-4-3-2.

Okay, so these numbers can't have anything to do with an address. I doubt he'd want me to add them together; that would be too-easy math. But I do it, anyway.

Seventeen.

Still, it can't be an address. The first number on this block is 100, and the numbers are going up.

Two men in ties are patting their faces with the backs of their hands at the exact same time.

A kid flies by on a bicycle, going downhill against traffic.

A rich lady, all dressed in white, is walking her so-tiny dog that looks like a rat.

And all I can do is stand here, sweating, and hope something pops out at me.

8-4-3-2.

I got nothing.

How did I go from giddy to miserable in less than fifteen minutes? My heart can't take this. I shouldn't have done it. This is not how it was meant to be. The riddles were never supposed to make you feel bad. They were supposed to be fun. Lukas wouldn't have made it this hard on purpose, because he'd have been here to point me in the right direction.

I'm hot.

I'm thirsty.

I let my knees buckle, and I slide my back against the wall till I'm squatting, and holding back my tears.

I just want to go home.

"Are you all right, young lady?"

When I look up, it's the lady with the rat dog. She seems nice, and I instantly feel bad for thinking that about her dog, even if up close, it looks even more like a rat.

I scramble to my feet and wipe at my face at the same time.

"Oh yeah. I'm fine."

"Is there anyone you can call?"

Before I can tell her I don't have my phone, she is holding hers out to me. It's all blinged out with green rhinestones, but so what?

"Thanks," I say. "I guess I could call my dad, if you don't mind."

"I'd feel better than leaving you here on the street, crying."

"I wasn't . . ." But, of course, I was.

"Go ahead. Just call." Her little dog sits down and pants, and they both turn their heads, as if they are giving me my privacy. "It's not locked," she adds.

"Thanks."

I press the telephone icon at the bottom, and a keypad appears on the screen.

Underneath the numbers are sets of three letters. Under the 2, there is *ABC*. Under the 3, *DEF*.

It wasn't a building number or address. Lukas was spelling something!

8-4-3-2.

Under the 8, there is *TUV*.

Under the 4, *GHI*, and under the 3, the only vowel is *E*.

The word *THE* comes to me.

But there's still another number: *2*. And under that, the letters *ABC*.

Not *THE*.

THEA.

I think I know the name Thea.

It's the lady who owns the shop where Lukas's mother brings their old clothes and stuff sometimes. I went there with them once. It's a consignment shop on Main Street. Halfway up the block, halfway down, and right across the street from where I am standing right at this very moment. I almost drop this most bedazzled cell phone.

"Oh, hey, look, thank you. Thank you, anyway, but I just remembered something. Something really important. I don't need to use your phone, but thank you, anyway. You are very nice. And so is your dog. Your dog is really cute." I'm blabbering and stammering, and I thrust the phone back into her hands. "I gotta go."

But I do remember to look before I dart across the street. I lift my eyes to the sign I hoped would be here, and there it is:

ANGEL'S ANTIQUES AND CONSIGNMENTS

When I push open the door, a little bell over my

head jangles, a whoosh of cold air greets me, and my relief is so much more than I'd let myself believe could be true.

I found where Lukas put the next clue.

We did it.

LUKAS

BY THE TIME I REACH THE BIG PICTURE WINDOW IN FRONT OF Angel's, where Thea works, I'm sweating, not just from the heat, but because I'm thinking about the pendant I bought for Joy again. What did Justin say this morning? *Nothing ruins a friendship like declaring your undying love?*

I am not doing that, though. (Am I?) I just know Joy likes nice hearts.

Still, as I think about it, my stomach twists, and twists some more about the note. My words there, the way I re-wrote it this morning. Maybe I should rip it up and start again, write what I always write: *Happy birthday, Joy. From your best friend, Lukas.* Because even that night, watching stars, Joy had said, *I wish we could always be friends.* She didn't say, *I wish we could be more than that. I wish you could think of me that other way.*

A drip of sweat slides down by my ear, because I also keep remembering how she squeezed my fingers under the sleeping bag that night, but I shouldn't think about that now.

There's a weird, muffled noise, someone yelling my name, and that someone is waving at me through the big front window. Thea, I think, but it's hard to tell with the glare.

"Hold on a second!" I say, because my phone is buzzing inside my pocket. It's Justin, texting to say they're heading out on the water, so I may not be able to reach him. "Be good," he writes, but I probably should text that to him. He needs to remember it more than I do.

"I will be," I text back, anyway. "Saw Jairo. He says hi."

I shove my phone away and stare down the hill toward Vincent's, using the bottom of my T-shirt to wipe the sweat from my face and neck. I could have made this a lot easier if I hid all the clues in one place. But I wanted this one to be special, since it's our fifth one ever, so it needed to be the kind of thing you remember even when you're old.

You should trust me on this, Justin had said, but he only knows how him and his friends are with girls, girls they're not even friends with in the first place. Girls you like from the get-go, then kiss, then decide a week later you don't like so much after all. That's nothing like Joy and me.

Another night I've been thinking about—a recent one—comes back to me, even though I've been trying not to think of it too much. It was only a few weeks ago. We were watching *Coraline* at Joy's house, and when the "One, two, three!" scene came on, Joy grabbed my hand and buried her face in my shoulder, even though she's seen the movie a whole bunch of times already. And when she finally let go, she left her hand sitting there on my knee.

I swear, it nearly burned a hole through my jeans.

After a few minutes, she realized it was there, I guess, and said, "Sorry!" and moved it. Even if I didn't want her to. I should have told her to keep it there.

I shake my head at my own stupidness and pull the door open, relieved for the cool, musty distraction of Thea's.

This is just some of what you see if you walk into Angel's Consignments: ugly lamps with yellow shades and nautical bases; ugly pillows with shiny braided ropes and dark stains, propped on mustard-and-red plaid armchairs with all their threads sticking out; wood and metal stools and tables, some in good shape, others kind of broken; books everywhere; boxes and boxes of doorknobs and glass drawer pulls and old-looking hardware and tools; pink and red and amber drinking glasses, with raised dots on the outsides like Braille, which someone's great-grandma must have used; a whole shelf full of tin policemen and tin carousels and tin circus clowns with dogs, waiting to be wound up to bark and clap and spin and march across the floor; and an old suit of armor that never leaves the corner, a rainbow of bright-colored feathered thingies wrapped around its neck. Boas. That's what Thea once told me they're called.

There are also cabinets full of jewelry made of clunky fake (I'm pretty sure) diamonds, and pink and yellow plastic stones, and whole racks of raincoats and fancy dresses, with beads and sparkly sequins, and men's sweaters and suits that have all started to smell kind of funky. And underneath them, along the floor, all sorts of shoes that have been worn before, from ladies' heels, to kids' sneakers, to men's dress shoes like Dad used to wear when he left for work in the mornings. Everywhere you look, there is something old waiting to be something new for someone.

"Well, hello, Mr. Brunetti!" Thea appears right next to me out of nowhere, making me jump out of my skin. "I thought I saw you outside!" she says, taking hold of my shoulders. Her breath smells sweet and powdery, and she studies me with her purple-blue eyes. "How the heck are you? Haven't seen you or that beautiful mama of yours in eons. How is she? And what brings you into this stuffy old place on a gorgeous summer day?"

That's a whole slew of questions, so I'm not sure which to answer first. I like Thea, but she sure can talk too much. She knows us because this is where we brought all of Dad's stuff after he died. Not right away, of course, because we wanted to keep it around to remind us of him, but then it just started to feel sad, plus we needed the money, plus we were selling the house, so Mom was ready to get rid of it all. Suits. Shoes. Watches. Boxes of the true-life biographies, and war and history books he liked to read. That was back when we lived in our own house, with a view of the water, but only from the attic if you went up there. Justin says Dad said he and Mom were going to open up the attic and make it their bedroom one day, but that was before he got sick. Back when he still worked for the bank in the city, and we had enough money to buy stuff we didn't absolutely need.

Justin remembers it all, but I don't, because I was not even six when we moved to the rentals so Justin and me could stay in our schools. Which is most important, because otherwise it would have been even worse for Justin, and I wouldn't have been best friends with Joy.

Anyway, because we were still little back then, Mom had to take us everywhere with her, including Thea's. So we took trip after trip here, dragging his things that had value. Once, when Mom came in with the box of Dad's shiny dress shoes, Thea said, "Are you sure you want to get rid of these, Melissa? Maybe the boys want to—"

But Mom cut her off. "No point in that, Thea. What good will it do any of us to keep holding on to his shoes?"

Sometimes Mom still has us run things over here to Thea's. A few months ago, Mom sold a ring that Rand gave her.

Justin and me were the ones who brought the ring over, and I could see how sad being at Thea's still makes him, because while Thea was examining the ring, Justin was staring at the row of cufflinks, his eyes all watery, which made me wonder if maybe he saw a pair he thought belonged to Dad. Anyway, the ring ended up fetching a whole $250, and so even though Mom said Rand would never spend that kind of money on her, he did, because the three small diamond chips were real.

"Go figure," Mom had said, with a big sad sigh, when Thea called to tell her to pick up the money.

And that was exactly the thing about Rand that made him so hard to be mad at: he could drink too much and be a jerk, but he could also take you out fishing or give you a nice diamond ring. He wasn't all good or all bad.

"She's fine. She's at work," I say now, wanting to answer at least one of the questions Thea puked out at me. "At the diner. And Justin is out in the *Angler* with a friend. The inflatable boat, I mean." I try to look at her as I talk, to be respectful, but my eyes are also busy scoping out the place, because I need to find somewhere safe but noticeable to hide the next clue. Something that will mean something special to Joy.

"Ah, well, that's good to hear. You boys do love the water, don't you? And a little hard work never hurt anyone, don't you agree?"

I look back at Thea and nod. Only then do I fully notice the weird little hat she's wearing, light purple felt with blue-and-green feathers, feathers that belong to a sequined peacock that struts along its edge.

Only Thea could wear a hat like that and get away with it. I mean, no offense, but she's a little weird, but in a fun way. She has gray hair she dyes too-bright red, and she wears stretchy pants covered in flowers, or old jeans covered with a hundred different patches, like peace signs and rainbow hearts and birds. And there's a sweet powder smell every time you walk too close to her.

"You like it?" she asks, watching my face and tapping the hat, then nods to a wooden rack covered with more colorful hats way over against the far wall. "A bunch more just came in. Someone who used to own a specialty hat shop and had these all in his basement for years. But this one, this one is a real beaut." Thea twirls like she's modeling. "Vintage pillbox with faux pearls, sequins, even a bridal veil," she adds, pulling a lavender net that's tucked somewhere behind the hat down over her eyes. "A stunner, don't you think? I've taken to wearing a different one every day since he dropped them off, just for the fun of it. It's for sale if you want it. Only three dollars. Two for you, because you're my guy."

I nearly start laughing, because why on earth would I ever want to own a peacock hat? But also because it's so perfect. The most perfect place ever to stash the next clue. Perfect because of Dana Arlington and her know-it-all self correcting me and Joy one day during a group project in Mr. McKenna's class last year.

"Just so you all know," Dana instructed, in this fake teachery voice, "a group of peacocks isn't called peacocks. Peacocks are just the males. Peahens are the females. So if you're referring to them *all*, you mean pea*fowl*."

61

That alone almost made me die laughing, but then I looked over at Joy, and she looked back at me, and then she turned back to Dana Arlington, all innocent.

"I'm confused," she said. "Which are the boy ones again? The hens?"

And Dana was so busy being smart, she didn't realize, and said, "No, the cocks are the boys, and hens are the girls, and you can remember it because, as with chickens, the girls are the hens."

"Oh right, great," Joy had said. "So *that's* how you can remember it?" By then I was bent over laughing, like, practically peeing my pants, and Dana was nodding, all proud for having taught us all something, until she suddenly caught on to us laughing, since Joy had slunk so far down in her chair, she was practically on the floor.

After that, no matter what, Joy and I only referred to peacocks as *peafowl*, always asking pretend-confused after, "But is the boy the cock or the hen?" which you'd think wasn't so often, because who talks about peacocks all that much? But for weeks after, we did. We stuck the word *peafowl* into everything we said, which was, sure, immature, but funny as heck, so we couldn't help ourselves.

"So, did you want it?" Thea asks, pulling a pin from the side of the hat. She lifts it off her head and holds it out to me.

I wish I could. Seriously. I wish I had two dollars, and maybe a tip to pay her for helping me out, but I don't, because I spent it all on the pendant, and, anyway, I only want to borrow the hat, not own it. I want it to stay in the shop and hide the clue, maybe in a spot in the window.

I take a deep breath. "I can't buy it today, Thea," I say. "But I'm wondering something else. Do you think you could do me a great big favor?"

6

JOY

IT'S HARD TO TELL AND I CAN'T BE SURE, BUT I THINK THIS IS the same woman from the time I was here with Lukas and his mom.

Thea.

I don't really remember what that lady looked like, except she wore crazy clothes. I do remember that, and this woman is wearing tight, faded denim overalls, with a red-and-white-striped leotard underneath and several strands of colorful beads around her neck. Her jet-black hair most definitely had to come out of a box of Clairol.

Thea?

Can you please tell me?

Is this Thea?

I guess she is.

But maybe she's the owner and her name is not Thea, but Angel, as in Angel's Consignments.

Or maybe she's really an angel.

"Can I help you?" she says. Her voice is deep and husky. I remember that, too.

I resist the urge to turn and head right back out. Only I've come this far, which really wasn't very far, but it still feels huge. And as hard as it is to imagine there is anything here for me, I have to be brave. I have to look.

Ask for her by name,

8-4-3-2.

I have to ask. "Are you Thea?"

She nods.

"I'm Lukas's friend," I say. "Lukas Brunetti? Do you remember me?"

She has a blank sort of look on her face.

"I'm Joy," I say.

It sounds so strange to hear my name out loud, even if it's me saying it. Which is strange, since I am plenty used to people using my name as a word.

"Joy to the World."

Joyride.

Jump for joy, that one gets me a lot of teasing.

Our bundle of joy.

You name it, I've heard it.

But I'm not joy. I mean, I *am* Joy, but I haven't been joy-*ful* in a long time.

"Lukas's friend . . ." She says it slowly. "Lukas Brunetti . . . And you're Joy?"

Even though I've just told her that. I say, "Yeah, I'm Joy Fonseca."

My answer suddenly sends her into a bustle of activity, like she's just stepped on a nest of red ants, which I've done before, by the way. "Yes, yes. I remember now." She's waving her arms around.

When she moves, a spray of dust and a hint of lilac lift into the air. "It has to be here somewhere."

She points. "I had it there. In the window for so long, then of course it was the hurricane and I had to move everything. I mean, the whole downtown, remember? We didn't know what was going to happen with the seawall and everything. Wasn't that something? A superstorm, they called it. We seem to be having them a lot these days."

As she is talking—I assume to *me*—she is opening and closing cabinets, running her hand over the top shelf of a stand-up wardrobe, lifting the lid off a big round box made of fabric. "I wasn't sure what to do with it . . . after . . . afterwards, if I should even mention it. It just didn't ever seem like a good time, but I do know I put it somewhere for safekeeping."

"So it is here? I *am* in the right place?" I start slowly, but I feel like I still need to ask. "You *are* Thea, then?"

She stops fluttering about and looks right at me. "Oh yes, sweetheart. And you're here for the note from Lukas

Brunetti, right?" Her voice catches on his name. "I know his mom well. I know both of them. I mean, all three of them, but I've known Melissa for a long time. She's good people. She always did right by her boys. More loss than any one woman should have to bear, but she's strong. She'll be okay. So will Justin."

So I've come to the right place; I found the third clue, but this time I don't feel the same elation. It's too personal in here, too close. I don't want to talk about Lukas; I just want to find the clue and get out of here. I'm not sure I want to hear about him from someone else, either.

Thea keeps talking. "This is a funny business, you know, so personal. I mean, when people are selling their stuff, it usually is, but then I have these things, and I feel a responsibility. People need the money, but sometimes I think it's more than that. No matter how much you give away, memories stick around, inside the lining of a coat or in the design of a salad bowl or on the pages of an old book. Memories stick around, even when you are trying to forget them."

"So Lukas *did* leave something for me?"

"Oh right, yes. The note. The note. It's been so long . . . but, of course, you know that." Thea lets her eyes rest on me for a split second, as if she's worried she's hurt my feelings or said the wrong thing, then she looks away, rummaging through a basket of scarfs and feather boas, even though I can tell she doesn't think she'll find what she is

67

looking for in there. I get it. I make people uncomfortable, or I make them nervous. Like, seeing me reminds them of something they don't want to be reminded of.

"I mean, can I help?" I say quickly. "Maybe if I knew what you were looking for?"

"Well, isn't that the sixty-four-thousand-dollar question?"

"Huh?"

"The old game show?"

I shake my head.

"Well, never mind, let me just think here a minute. . . . I know it was a . . ." Thea reaches her hands up in pantomime, as if something were there. Big hair? A towel? As if she is putting something on her head.

"A hat?" I try.

"Yes, that's it. Lukas wanted to put the note in the hat, just for one day, so of course I told him he could. But it had to be this one particular hat, he said. It couldn't be any other one." She's moving around the store again. "Please don't worry, sweetheart. It's here. I didn't sell it. Not so many takers, with all those huge peacock feathers."

Lukas, you didn't?

"A hat with feathers?"

"Yes, a purple pillbox with peacock feathers and faux pearls," Thea says, and she turns her attention right to me. "Why, do you see it?"

I swear, if I could feel laughter molecules in the air,

they'd be speeding up like water heating in a pot, bubbling to the surface, popping right in front of my face. I ask very slowly, very carefully, "So we're looking for a purple hat with . . ." I can't bring myself to say it. "Feathers?"

Lukas always knew what would make me laugh, the kind of laugh that gets you in trouble, the kind of laughing when you aren't supposed to be laughing. The kind you can't stop. The more you want to, the less you can.

Only that's all gone now.

But then she goes and says it again.

"It's purple felt, with three beautiful"—Thea draws her fingers back, along the side of her head, demonstrating how long they were—"antique peacock feathers."

And it's suddenly all in front of me: Lukas, Dana Arlington, Mr. McKenna. Dana's smug face, Lukas's sideways glance in my direction. And, oh my God, I nearly peed in my pants. I had to hold my stomach, it hurt so much from laughing, and for weeks and weeks after that, we didn't let the joke go.

Me (giving Lukas the perfect setup as we stood in the lunch line): Hey, Lukas, you getting chicken nuggets today?

Lukas: No. Today's special. Peafowl.

Me (trying not to laugh): Which fowl? Boy fowl or girl fowl?

Lukas: Definitely not . . .

Before we get any of the rest of the words out, both of us fall over laughing, with everyone around us looking at us.

69

And then somehow I realize I've been saying this all out loud. To Thea. And I'm not crying. I'm laughing.

"I can see why you two were such good friends. Same sense of humor. It's what kept me and my hubby together these thirty-five years," she says, and after a beat, she adds, "I'm sure it wasn't his good looks."

And we both crack up at that one.

"Wait, I remember." Thea jumps up off the velvet couch as best she can in those tight overalls. "Good looks! That's it. I remember where I put it."

I follow her.

"I put it behind the full-length mirror, the foggy one with all the scratches and chips. Here, here it is, right back here." She bends down and carefully reaches her hand behind a giant stand-up mirror that is leaning against the far wall.

"Can you believe Anthropologie is selling a brand-new one made to look all worn like this one for sixteen hundred dollars?"

When she stands, her knees crack loudly, but she is holding the hat, and when she reaches inside the hat, there is another note, folded neatly inside, and it has my name on top.

Just like the last one.

LUKAS

"HEY, LUKAS?"

"Yeah, Rand?"

It's a Sunday morning, the first summer Rand is living with us, so I'm almost ten and Justin is fourteen, and Rand and me are walking down to the marina to go fishing. Usually it's all three of us, Justin, Rand, and me, but this morning, it's only us two.

We left our apartment while it was practically still dark out, but we stopped for breakfast sandwiches from the deli that opens super-early, so now, as we head to the marina, the day is starting to get lit up by the sun. Even though that makes me feel cheerier, I'm still wishing Justin came along. I like it better when all three of us are together, but Justin was too tired this morning, because now that he's in high school, Mom lets him stay out until midnight on Saturdays.

We head toward the marina, me carrying the food and a coffee can of worms, and Rand carrying the tackle box, our rods tucked up under his arm. We'll eat, then fish, and

71

later go up to B&B's to get better lures, and check out the new rods and reels.

"Hey, Lukas?" Rand asks again, like I missed something.

"Yeah?" I answer again, because my brain may be busy, but I'm listening. We round the corner toward Shore Road and take the path down, gravel crunching under our feet.

"Where do fish keep their money?"

I knew it! At first I thought he was going to ask something serious, but then I figured, probably not. Probably just some dumb Rand joke. Because that's a thing he does, tells me dumb fish jokes all the time.

Like, Question: How do shellfish get to the hospital?

Answer: They call a clambulance.

But now I'm thinking and thinking, and nothing is coming to me. I say, "I don't know, Rand. Where *do* fish keep their money?"

"In a riverbank, dumbo."

"Ha, ha, ha," I answer, because it's lame but also funny, and after that, I don't talk much because Rand walks fast, with his tall, tall self and long, long legs, and his Timberland boots he always wears, with the orange PRO tags, going *clump-clump-clump* on the pavement. Two steps of mine to every one of his, so I have to concentrate to keep up with him.

Finally we reach the marina, and Rand sits on a bench, and I sit next to him, and we wolf down our sandwiches and throw the wrappers in the garbage, and then Rand walks to the very edge of the first boat slip and stands, drinking his coffee, no words or jokes, just sipping and watching the cormorants lined up on the floating docks, and the boats bobbing up and down near their mooring balls.

I don't talk, either, just get up and stand next to him, because I don't want to disturb him. I think about stuff, too, stuff I wouldn't say, like how I sometimes wish that Rand was my father.

I know I shouldn't wish it. Justin gets mad at me if I do, because he doesn't like Rand the way I do. He doesn't hate him, not exactly, but he remembers our real dad completely and he doesn't think Rand is good "father material." Mostly because of how Rand lies about beers and drinking them when he's not supposed to. And then Mom yells, and Rand yells back, and Mom cries and says it's dangerous to us, and Rand promises he'll stop drinking and get help.

Once, for like two whole months, he did get help, went to meetings and stuff, and everything got better for a while. Then he crashed his truck, and it turned out he didn't tell us about how he had stopped going to the meetings, but this time he swore he wanted to fix things. He promised he'd do it for good.

"Too late," Mom said. "Don't come back until you've got a whole lot of meetings under your belt."

But this is before that, and he's not drinking beer at all

this morning. He's drinking coffee and telling jokes, and we're both looking out over the water. And he sure seems like good father material when we're doing this.

"Hey, Rand?" I finally say when he tips the blue-and-white cup back to polish off the last dregs of coffee. We grab our stuff again and start walking to the quiet end of the marina. The end down by Gooseneck Bridge.

"Yes, Lukas?"

I concentrate hard so I don't mess it up, because I suddenly remembered this joke out of nowhere.

"What's the best way to catch a fish?"

Rand turns to me, one eyebrow raised. He hands me a rod, and I kneel and open the can full of worms and pull one out and hold my breath while I stick the hook through its soft, squishy middle. In my head I whisper, "Sorry, worm, sorry," then wipe my hands on my pants, and watch as a seagull swoops down, landing on the mast of the big pretty sailboat called *YOLO*. It squawks at us, mad and demanding, wanting a worm for itself.

"I don't know, kiddo," Rand says. "I give up. What's the best way to catch a fish?"

I stand up again and show him my baited hook, and he nods.

"Have someone throw it to you," I say.

It takes a second for the big goofy smile to crack across Rand's lips, and the seagull squawks again like it got the joke, too, and Rand puts his head back and laughs and laughs and laughs.

✳

I work my way down Main Street toward the marina and B&B's, wishing so many things, but mostly that Joy were here with me. But of course she's not. She can't be. Because that would ruin everything.

The best thing about Joy is that she's funny, and the worst thing about these scavenger hunts is that we do this part, the setting up, alone. If she were with me, we'd be laughing and talking and she'd be skipping ahead, wrinkling her nose, and saying, "Oh no, not the bait shop, do not make me go in there! That place smells like dead fish!" And I'd kick rocks—once, the same rock all the way from our apartment to the start of the gravel path down to the marina—and my brain wouldn't be thinking about things like Rand being father material and then leaving.

But tomorrow, it will be worth it. I know it will. When Joy sees what I've done, and all the effort.

It'll be special. Perfect. And the heart pendant will be waiting for her at the end.

That, and the note.

If I leave the note.

But I'm leaning toward probably I will.

I think some more about tomorrow morning as I move

toward the row of shops across from the harbor, walking through the steps in my head.

I'll get up super-early and drop the first clue under her door. Then I'll wait for her to finish her big Fonseca Family Birthday Breakfast Bash and find it. When she figures it out and gets to Vincent's, I'll be waiting outside for her. Then I'll go with her to the rest of the stops. But I won't help her. Lips sealed. She'll have to figure out where I hid each next clue herself.

As for the Fonseca Family Birthday Breakfast Bash, it's not that I'm not invited, because I could go. They tell me I should every year. But it's a special family thing, and I like to let them have it alone. Otherwise, I'd just feel like they feel sorry for me, and that's why they invite me to come. Joy says, "No, Lukas, not true, we like having you here," but sometimes I remember more than she does that her family used to want her to stay away from me. That me and Mom and Justin seemed like trouble.

"That was because of Justin, not you," she reminds me all the time. "And you gotta admit that Justin has gotten into his fair share of trouble. But they didn't know you back then, and now they do, and they get why you're amazing, just like I do."

But Justin is still my brother and I love him, so I don't always feel so much better about things.

Anyway, after dinner, they'll have me over for cake, and

that will be fine, because Isabel and Davy like me a ton, and cake is the most important thing.

Once Isabel pops into my head, it hits me where to hide the red box with the note and the pendant, because it has to be right near Joy's apartment: in the fake potted plant outside the Fonsecas' front door, where Isabel hides whenever she knows I'm coming over. Me and Joy laugh so hard when Isabel hides there and thinks we can't see her, since the plant is taller than she is. She doesn't understand that I can still see her squatting back there because we're looking at her from above.

I walk faster until the backs of the buildings down on Shore Road come into view, and the tall masts of the sailboats, and the tops of the trees that circle around the park and keep the gazebo in shade.

Our local marina is much busier than the dock at the Point. It's surrounded by a surf shop, a taco place, a restaurant that lets you sit out on the pier in the summertime, B&B's, and a few other shops. The dock at the Point is only for fishermen, basically just a pier with some boat slips, where clammers and fishing boats leave off from. Along the beach is a series of small, mostly abandoned docks made from broken pier planks that were hauled into the marshy area and are now overgrown with grasses and cattails. People made them to keep their kayaks, and stuff that got too big for the car, but after a while the weather and water made the docks hard to get to. One of those is where we hide the *Angler* and the motor, the dock where Chance and Justin will have pushed off from.

As I walk toward B&B's, it's that dock I'm thinking about, and about Chance and Justin and what they're doing now. They've probably motored out to the middle of the bay.

I wish I were out there, too, nothing but water, my head tipped back, pops of sunlight bouncing off the surface, twinkling all around me like sparkler bits.

I don't even need to be fishing to be entertained. I could just sit and watch the sea robins flick their tails, their big stupid ears flopping up out of the water like Dumbo fish. Or the goofy cormorants lined up on the floating docks, their orange beaks like a row of sideways traffic cones, a bunch of naked penguins who forgot their fancy tuxedo suits.

Sometimes, if Mom and Rand were having a fight, I'd say I was going for a bike ride, then I'd go all those miles down the causeway and pull out the *Angler* by myself, and take it for a spin around the harbor. I'd get looks for sure, like the grown-ups were suspicious of me having no permission. But I always stayed close to shore and pretended Rand was watching out for me on the pier. I'd even fake-wave to him, even though no one was there. Besides, strangers would be able to tell, from the way I handled the *Angler* and had all the right gear, that I know what I'm doing out there. So nobody ever ratted me out or told me I needed to go back to shore.

I finally reach the door to B&B's and slip in quick, deciding not to bother asking for permission to hide the clue. It's not like I'm stealing, only touching things and leaving something, and there are five people lined up at the register. I'd have to wait my turn to ask, and it's already later than I want it to be.

I walk to the reel displays, casual-like, and quick-wedge the fourth clue under the shiny red Revo Rocket display model they put out last week, leaving just the tiniest bit of white corner sticking out.

My heart pounds from nervousness.

Head down and nonchalant, I move toward the door.

Clue #4 is now planted.

As I slip out the door and into the sunlight again, a hand grabs my shoulder and squeezes hard.

"Mr. Brunetti?" its voice booms, stopping me there in my tracks.

7

JOY

I HAVE THE THIRD CLUE IN MY HANDS NOW, BUT INSTEAD OF feeling grateful or satisfied, I just keep thinking I might be able to find the next one. I won't let myself wish past that.

Just one more.

One more would be enough.

But it's also becoming increasingly obvious I am not going to make it home close to any reasonable time, and if my parents haven't called the Rogers yet, they will soon. And when they do that, their next call will be to the Port Bennington Police Department.

Out of the corner of my eye, just as I think this, I see a police car turning onto Shore Road. I swear, it's slowing down. Any second, I'm going to hear a siren and see flashing lights, but it makes another left and disappears. Still, I need to call home.

And I need to pee.

And I'm really hungry.

It's quieter down here, and I'm calmer now. The farther down Main Street I get, the quieter it gets. It takes me another ten minutes or so of walking before I am far enough away from the Dunkin' and Lang's Pharmacy to really catch my breath. Right where Main Street turns into Shore Road, the marina and the bait-and-tackle shop are just ahead.

It's the smell that hits you first, mud and fish and worms. Low tide, I guess.

But it is cooler here; there's a breeze off the water.

The "where" part of Lukas's next clue is so easy, too easy.

> Head to a place
> I like more than you.

Anybody who knew Lukas, and knew me, could guess what this clue meant.

B&B Sport and Tackle.

I had been there a bunch of times with Lukas so he could pick up whatever gear he said he needed, or a Tupperware of live bait for fishing, but I think he just likes taking me there. He likes scaring me with the rubbery, fake grubs.

Everything down here by the marina is smaller: the taco shop, the place my mom and dad like to go for fried clams so they can look out on the water. It's where the locals moor their boats or come to fish, or drop their nets for bay scallops when they don't want to go out into the open water, when they want to get away from the noisy summer-rental people who mostly fish off Gooseneck Bridge. And there's B&B's.

I feel like I might be able to pee right behind this abandoned pier and no one would see me unless they were walking along the dune over there. Maybe a few feet ahead would be better. I really have to go. But hopefully they have a bathroom inside this place. Then a phone. And then whatever it is Lukas was trying to tell me with the clue he left in the purple felt hat.

He wrote it out so carefully:

> Look for the Rocket.
> You'll reel in a clue.

I can practically hear his voice reciting:

> Head to a place
> I like more than you.
> Look for the Rocket.
> You'll reel in a clue.

It doesn't mean the clue is still here, but it does mean I'm in the right place. I'm sure of it, and now that I've started this, I have no choice. I have to see where it takes me.

Gee, thanks, Lukas, for taking me here.

Bait shops like this open super-early, and sometimes they close early, too, so I'm not sure when I pull on the rickety door, hung with miniature red-and-white buoys, if it will open.

But it does.

First things first.

"Do you have a bathroom I could use?" I ask.

Without looking up from the comic he's flipping through, the boy behind the counter answers me with "Can't you read?"

It takes me a minute, but I figure it out before he decides to explain. "The sign. On the door," he grunts.

RESTROOM FOR CUSTOMERS ONLY! ! !

There are big handwritten signs like this all over Port Bennington. They go up in storefront windows starting around May 1, and they don't come down until well into October. I get it. They don't want people coming in and out all day, just messing up their bathrooms, using all their soap and paper towels, and then heading off to the beach without buying anything.

"Look," I say. "I'm having a hard day, and I'm not some tourist. I live here, and I really need to use the bathroom. So I am just going to find it myself."

I don't think I've ever been so mean to a stranger before. I instantly regret it, but at least the boy finally lifts his head, and I see he's not really a kid, more like a teenager, maybe, like, Natalia's age. He opens his mouth, probably to slam me with something much nastier than I could ever come up with, but when he sees me, he doesn't.

Maybe he's surprised to see I'm not some annoying little kid.

"It's there." He points to the back of the shop, to a wall of shelves, stacked with coolers of all sizes, and a door posted with another sign: STAFF ONLY. I speed-walk toward it and straight inside.

There's a little mirror over the sink in this tiny bathroom. There's also an empty, upside-down bucket of what was once frozen trolling cut bait, several fishing nets hanging up to dry, and a few poles, without any reels, leaning against the wall. So when I'm done, I step over a puddle of unknown substance to wash my hands, and I look up at my reflection.

I free the stray hairs that are stuck to my sweaty face and try a big smile, with lots of teeth. Nah, looks too forced. I try another, kind of a slow lift, more on the right side of my mouth, lips closed this time, to see how that looks.

I try one more practice smile, maybe a nice mix of the two. I go back to Smile One.

Yeah, I think that's better.

Or Two.

I kind of feel like I'm Natalia, barricaded in the bathroom for a ridiculously long time every morning, taking far more than her share of the time, staring at her face in the mirror. It drives us all crazy.

But sometimes, if I bug her enough, bang on the door, threaten to tell, she lets me sit on the side of the tub, and I watch her do her hair, sweeping it up into a ponytail that is loose and soft but somehow stays in place, high and tight. Then she paints a black line on her top eyelid, drawn to a perfectly skinny point. And she smacks pink gloss onto her lips.

She leans down and dabs a bit on me. "Don't tell Ma," she whispers. "But you do look pretty."

And with that thought comes another rush of an unwanted feeling wrapped inside an unwanted memory. This time I hold fast, meeting my own gaze in the mirror and not letting it go.

I close my eyes and kiss the air in front of the mirror.

Did you hear what I said? On the phone? The last time we talked?

Okay, okay, snap out of it, I tell myself.

I need to concentrate on figuring out what Lukas wanted me to find, which means I need to buy myself more time in here, which means I'm going to have to call home right away. I take another deep inhale, exhale, and start to formulate a series of what-ifs.

What if my dad answers the phone?

What if my mom does?

But then again, the smartest move would be if I just call Natalia's cell phone. And if I don't want the state troopers to find me before I find this rocket, or *the* Rocket, I'd better do whatever it is I have to do fast.

I head back up front to the counter, where the boy seems

not to have budged one inch, and I try Smile Two. "Thanks for letting me use the bathroom, and by the way, do you have a phone I could use?"

He is just staring at me.

I switch to Smile One and add, "I need to call my sister."

Very slowly, he reaches behind the counter, lugs out a heavy, black, old-fashioned phone, which looks like it hasn't been used since the 1990s, and plops it on the counter. "Sure."

And I realize I'm not sure I know Natalia's number.

While my mind is working on that—*what is her number?*—my eyes wander around the hundreds of things for sale in here, thousands of things on the shelves, millions of things hanging on the walls, the posters for outboard motors, the local advertisements for full- and half-day fishing excursions. How will I ever know what Lukas wanted me to find?

It's overwhelming.

> *Look for the Rocket.*
> *You'll reel in a clue.*

There is so much in this place, knives and lures and nets and buckets and fishing rods and fishing reels. What did he write? *Reel in a clue.* A reel! *Rocket* with a capital *R*. Of course. It must be some special kind of fancy reel—the thing that goes on the fishing pole, the part you crank around when you want to bring the hook back in.

With my hand still over the top of the phone—at least it has buttons and not a dial that you have to stick your finger in—my mouth blurts out, "Do you have a fishing reel called the Rocket?"

The boy's face kind of lights up, and I hope he's not taking this as a sign that I like fishing or anything. "Oh yeah, the Revo Rocket. Great reel. Not cheap, though. You looking for one?"

This hunt has taken on a life of its own. Every clue I find makes me want to find another. Makes me believe it might actually be possible. I can feel my heart quickening without permission, thunking, pounding on the inside of my ribs. I try to damp down my excitement and figure out the best way to go with this. I don't want to scare this guy away with my whole long story.

I've got to slow down. Be smart.

"Yeah, as a matter of fact, I am," I say, as calmly as I can, and just to make it more realistic, I add, "For my dad."

"Oh, wait," he says. "We had a ton of 'em at the beginning of the season—"

"Wait?" I interrupt. "What for?"

"Well, I can check, but we really sold a lot this year," the boy says. "I think we have this one left in the display." He turns around to where the wall behind him opens into a storefront window cluttered with nautical paraphernalia, and watching over it all is a carved wooden sailor with a pipe in his mouth. The boy moves some things around, then gives up pretty quickly.

"Oh, sorry. Guess we sold that one, too." He turns back around.

I am beginning to wonder if his confidence in my actual ability to pay for anything has something to do with his lack of effort. He barely searched. He barely tried.

It's got to be here.

"Can you just take another look around? The Revo Rocket." I say it slower and maybe a bit louder.

"I'm not hard of hearing," he says. "We ain't got 'em anymore."

Surely I am about to wear out my welcome. I think my smiles may have backfired completely. But this can't be how it ends. Not here, at Lukas's favorite place in the whole world. It doesn't make sense, in the crazy way none of anything in the world makes sense. But especially not this.

There has to be something here. I can feel it.

I think I even stamp my foot a little.

Where there's a will, there's a way, my dad always tells us.

"It's really important," I say to this frustratingly stubborn person behind the counter, and I wonder how much I can or should or *could* explain.

I'm sure he'd remember the story. Not about our scavenger hunt, of course, but it was big news, horrible news, for a while. Like a heavy hush that came over the locals and a rumor that went around with the tourists.

Not good for business, either.

So if this guy lived within twenty miles of here, he'd have heard, he'd know the name, he'd remember, and then he'd get that look on this face that everyone gets when they don't want to think about something.

But he wouldn't be able to help me. Nobody could.

"Are you sure?" I ask.

He is.

Sometimes there is a will, and no way.

And if the Rocket isn't here . . . it isn't here. There's nothing anyone can do about that.

Maybe it's better this way.

After all, it was a game; that's all it was. One clue to another to another, the fun was in the riddles. Sure, we tried to outdo each other with our own cleverness. But the real point was to hang out together. It didn't have any big meaning or conclusion.

My birthday, then Lukas's.

There isn't much else to do in Port Bennington over the summer, anyway. That's all it was. That's all this ever was, right?

I'll call Natalia and I'll go home. Happy birthday to me.

"I can order you one, if you want."

I shrug and say, "No thanks," while my whelm is quickly fading into defeat and I almost welcome it. If I got to the last clue, it would all be over, anyway, and nothing would change.

This way, I can hang on forever to not knowing.

LUKAS

"WHAT ARE YOU DOING HERE?" THE HAND SQUEEZES TIGHTER.

I don't look up. I didn't steal anything, but I did trespass, I guess. Acted like I had the right to go sticking clues under merchandise.

"Lukas?" The deep voice sounds familiar. I bring myself to look up. "It's nice to see you here. How's your summer going?"

It's not the owner scolding me for anything at all. My heart does a smile. It's Mr. Carter, from second grade.

I mean, I think it is. His black, curly hair is grayish now, and shorter, right to his head, while his face looks younger than I remember, which makes those two things contradictory. But when I look a little longer, he has the same eye-crinkling smile, and I definitely know the voice, so I'm sure. He holds a tackle box in his free hand. A white bucket, with a rod sticking out, sits next to him on the ground. He must be heading down to the marina.

A feeling of guilt washes over me. I always liked Mr. Carter and meant to go say hi to him but haven't seen him in so long because he's still in the elementary school, and Joy and me have been in the middle school for a whole year. And even before we moved to the middle school for sixth grade, the fourth and fifth grades were in a whole other wing from the lower grades. So unless he was on cafeteria duty or something, I didn't really run into him.

But here he is now, smiling, with his booming voice and big old hand on my shoulder. I look down, self-consciously for a second, then remember what he taught us and force myself to look back up at him again and hold my gaze there.

He nods, proud-like, and says, "So, now, a proper greeting," and holds his hand out to me to shake, and I nearly start laughing. Because now I remember this hilarious thing he used to do when we were in his class, when he was always teaching us things besides reading and math. Things he learned in the navy, he said, serving our country. Like always be polite, always walk with your head held up, and never ever look down like you're afraid. And when you're talking to someone, always look them sharp in the eyes. Speak clearly and slowly, with a purpose, and always, *always*, shake a new person's hand.

"Firm grip, like this, like you mean it." He'd demonstrate, holding his hand straight in mid-air to shake an invisible person's. Then he'd loosen his fingers and drop his wrist down, all floppy, and say, "None of this I'm-shaking-hands-with-a-dead-fish type of thing."

He was strict about it, too, and every once in a while, he would line us all up for a handshaking drill, and each of us would have to walk across the room to him, one at a time, head up, and say, "Hello, Mr. Carter, how are you?" looking him straight in the eye.

I bet a lot of kids forgot how he taught us that stuff, but I remember because it seemed so important to him that I learned. And here's the funny part: even though most of the time he was super-serious about it, sometimes, when you made it across the room and said, "Hello, Mr. Carter, how are you?" he would say, "I'm fine, Lukas, thanks for asking," and then he'd hold out his hand for you to shake. And if you were the lucky kid that day, instead of a normal, firm, navy handshake, you would get the Milk Shake Handshake, with Mr. Carter gripping your hand and making it jiggle up and down, up and down, a million miles per hour, so fast your arm looked like a crazy, vibrating rubber band. And if you opened your mouth to talk while he was shaking, your words would jiggle and vibrate, too, like someone was putting them through a washing machine.

"He-he-he-hel-lo, Mi-ih-ih-ih-ih-ster Ca-ah-ah-ah-ahr-ter," your words would go, and the best part would be you'd be laughing, but he'd act all serious and just keep shaking your hand, jiggling your arm all crazy fast, while saying, "Stop doing that, Lukas. Why are you doing that to me?" Only, of course, you weren't doing it, he was the one doing it, and you were the one laughing, while the next kid in line was anxiously waiting for her turn.

Now I'm grinning like a dope, staring at his hand like maybe he'll remember and Milk Shake Handshake me, but all he does is squeeze my hand warmly, two times, firmly, and say, "That's a nice strong grip you've got, Lukas."

He lets go. I feel a little disappointed.

"I'm good, sir," I say, not even sure he asked me.

"Well, glad to hear it, son. Very glad. You've grown some. I almost didn't recognize you."

And I don't know if it's my disappointment, or the way he's holding my stare like he really needs me to know how truly glad he is, or maybe because he called me son, but for a second I feel even worse about never going back to his classroom to visit.

"Sorry, Mr. Carter," I say when I've swallowed back the sad feeling and can look up again.

"It's okay, Lukas. Sometimes it's overwhelming to see old friends."

I wonder if that's true, and if an old teacher can actually become your real friend.

"Where were you headed? Maybe got a few minutes to sit?" He nods toward the end of the marina. "I was just going to do a little fishing. Fishing and meditation." He chuckles. "Half hour, tops. As you can see"—he taps his foot against the bucket—"it wasn't in my original plan this

94

morning, but I find myself with a canceled appointment, so I thought I'd dangle a line for a bit. Strictly catch and release. Never can bring myself to keep them, even to eat." He chuckles again, and I nod in agreement.

"Me neither. And, yeah, okay," I say, forgetting about time running out to get the hunt set, and already starting to walk with him.

8

JOY

NATALIA WILL BE HERE ANY MINUTE, BECAUSE SOMEHOW MY fingers remembered her cell number and pressed the right buttons, and she answered her phone before I even heard it ringing on my end. She wasn't exactly happy with me, but she wasn't so mad, either. She promised she'd smooth things over with our parents, and that, no, they hadn't contacted the police yet but, yes, I'd probably called just in the nick of time.

I told my sister where I was, and oddly she didn't ask why, which is probably because, since she got her driver's license last month, she'll take any excuse to borrow Dad's pickup. When I told her I'd wait for her outside B&B Sport and Tackle, all she said was that she'd be there in five minutes.

In Natalia Fonseca time, that could be twenty-five minutes to half an hour, but I don't care. I don't mind the wait.

The tide is starting to come in.

It swirls around the whole peninsula of Port Bennington, straight from the salty ocean and up onto every bay inlet and into the Sound and over the narrow strip of beach. It covers the black mud and creeps up to the watermarks on the pilings and the rocks. It swallows the green algae and laps gently at the sand.

I sit and swing my legs off the end of the pier. I'll be able to see Natalia when she pulls in. Meanwhile, I just need to be here for a minute more, with the sun on my face. There's a heron on the opposite side, walking its graceful stick walk in and out of the surf, just like nobody's business, and I know what it's telling me.

It's over.

No more clues.

"Time to go home," the heron would say, if it could talk.

"Hey, kiddo."

I spin around. It's not Natalia. It's a man in a white T-shirt and big belly.

"Yeah?"

The man waits at the foot of the pier. He doesn't come closer; instead he points back toward the tackle shop. "Patrick, my son. The boy you were talking to inside," he calls to me. "He said you were looking for something . . . for the Revo Rocket?"

Lukas once told me that there is an infinite number of moments in every second, that every second you can halve, and then halve again and again and again. There is still time left. It might be too small for our brains to comprehend, but it exists simply because of the math of it. And it is in one of those fractions of a moment of a second that I let myself get my hopes up.

Again.

"We are all sold out of those," the man tells me. "But maybe you were looking for *someone*, then?" He continues, "Maybe I know what you were looking for. That boy who used to come here all the time . . . I feel terrible about it now."

On the opposite side of the water, the heron lifts into the air.

"That Brunetti kid. He came in here that day . . . right before—" He stops, like he can't say the words. I get that.

"He went right for that same reel you were asking about, the Rocket. He had it in his hands. The one you were looking for . . . He came in so fast and dashed back out like he was up to no good. Like his brother, I figured. I figured he stole something. I was about to chase after him."

The heron hunches its shoulders, then spreads out its wings across the sky, past the sun, and lets its skinny legs dangle below.

"But then I saw him right outside, so I guess he wasn't running away or anything. I always felt bad about that, you know. Considering what happened. I just wanted to let you know. I always felt bad about it."

Higher and higher.

I just stare at the guy. He doesn't walk away.

"Anyways, then like a month or whatever later," he tells

me, "I go to sell that same Revo Rocket to some guy from Manhasset, and I see this little note underneath. And it's got a name on it."

"What name?"

The heron is almost out of sight.

"Look, I didn't think anything of it. I didn't even put two and two together till just now. Till you came along, asking for that same reel. It must be you, right? . . . Look, I didn't know, okay?"

It's a tiny dot against the blue.

The man shrugs, like he is casting off a heavy coat, one he's been wearing for too long. "I didn't know, I don't remember, so I threw it out. I'm sorry, okay? I really hope it wasn't anything important."

Smaller and smaller.

And it's gone.

I stand when I spot Natalia driving up in our dad's truck. She's got the windows down, her hair blowing behind her, and the music blasting. The man is already heading back into his shop. He looks helpless, or maybe it's me. Maybe I feel helpless.

At least my sister is here. I can tell her everything now. Now that it's over.

I start to head down the pier. *It's okay*, I tell myself. After the last whole year I've been through, this really isn't so bad. Nothing could be that bad. This is nothing compared to that.

99

Natalia shifts into park and waves at me. Then, just before I walk over to the passenger side and get in, the man in the white T-shirt calls out to me again.

He's standing in the doorway of his shop. "Hey, I don't know if this helps or anything. But I did see your friend talking with that black dude that always comes in here. I think he's a teacher from the elementary school."

"Mr. Carter?" I ask.

"Yeah, that's him. I saw him and that Brunetti kid talking, like, for a long time. Yeah, and they were fishing. Right outside. Right where you were just sitting."

I raise my hand to wave at him. "Thanks," I say back. Like I'm forgiving him.

And me.

LUKAS

THE SUN IS DOING THAT SPARKLE-POPCORN THING OFF THE water today, and maybe it's that, or maybe it's being with Mr. Carter that fills me with this feeling that everything is calm and good. I'm happy to be taking a break, sitting on the edge of the pier with him. Even if I'm also worried about slowing down and not getting the scavenger hunt finished. But I have plenty of time, and no one is at home to worry about me.

It must be heading toward low tide, because with our legs over the side, our feet dangling down, there's still a four- or five-foot drop to the water. Mr. Carter opens the tackle box, baits the line, and casts out. He hums for a minute, some song I don't know, then pulls back on the line and reels it in, slack and empty. Shaking his head, he casts out again.

"You have to be more patient than that," I say, and he laughs. "Give the fish a bit of time."

"Apparently, I'm a little rusty," he says. "I used to fish with my dad as a boy all the time, and now and again, as we both got older. He passed on a few years ago, and I haven't been out since . . . I find myself thinking a lot about him lately."

I nod, not sure what to say. Besides, I think I know what he's doing, because it's something else people do all the time: find ways to ask about my dad without really asking. Or maybe he knows about Rand. That now he's gone, too. Anyway, losing his dad is probably harder for him than it is for me, since he knew his father his whole lifetime, a whole lot longer than I knew mine. But I don't say that in case it sounds mean.

"I was doing a scavenger hunt just before," I blurt instead. "Setting one up, I mean. For Joy Fonseca. It's her birthday tomorrow. She was in your class, too, remember? She's my best friend now."

"Of course I remember Joy!" Mr. Carter says. He turns and looks at me, amused. "Go figure. Lukas Brunetti and Joy Fonseca. I wouldn't have pegged the two of you as lifelong friends." He winks at that, so I'm not sure what he's trying to tell me, but it doesn't matter because my brain is sticking on the word *lifelong*.

Here it goes, then. I wish we could always be friends.

"Well, we are," I say. "Lifelong best." And then I get that same squeeze in the pit of my stomach as I did when we were little and Joy's sister Natalia and her parents would watch me so, so closely every time I came over and hung out there. Like they were waiting for me to do something bad, take something that didn't belong to me. "Her and me," I add, to make a point, "have spent practically every day friends, ever since the last day of your class in second grade."

"She and I," Mr. Carter says, fixing my grammar, which makes my ears burn bright red. For a split second, I almost get mad, but then he says, "And however it happened, I'm glad to hear it. She was a smart girl. Good work ethic. She could almost keep up in math with the likes of you."

He yanks on the line, which is slack, so when he reels it in, of course the lure dangles, shiny, in the sun. He casts back out with a sigh. "So tell me about this scavenger-hunt thing."

I explain how we've been doing them since that summer right after his class, and how it kind of started with the cupcakes and both of us having cruddy summer birthdays. How, when we were little, we'd keep the hunts small and in one spot, but this year I wanted it to be special.

"I even got her this super-special necklace to find at the end—"

I stop there, my ears burning again, because even though I didn't say that it's a heart, or anything about the letter, or about me feeling stuff for Joy that maybe I'm not supposed to feel, whatever I did say makes Mr. Carter turn.

"You know," he says, his eyes twinkling, "if you still need a good hiding spot, I know the best one." He hands me the rod and stands, stretching his legs before cupping his hand to his eyes to stare off toward the park and the gazebo. "Look there." He points. "That tree in the center . . . It must be thirty years old now, because it was already big when we discovered it. . . . You see it there?"

I nod, not sure if I do.

"The heart-shaped tree, with the whale's eye . . . Even from here, you can see the top of it. . . ."

"The whale's eye?" I ask, not going near that heart part he's talking about.

"Yes, third from the gazebo, you see?" He points again, across the length of the marina, and down the long stretch of lawn toward where the big white gazebo sits in the center. In the summer, they have small concerts there. Mostly barbershop quartets, or even harpists sometimes. The area around the gazebo is circled with trees. "It's easier to see how it's heart-shaped in the fall, because now, in summer, its leaves are fuller. You see what I mean? You might have to stand up and squint."

I don't stand because I've got the line cast out and it feels like something might be biting, but while Mr. Carter keeps talking, I do count silently to try to see if I can tell which tree it is from here.

"So, back when the missus and I were still dating—now, granted, this was in high school, so I was still pretty smitten, though she will tell you I continue to be a hopeless romantic to this day—we used to do something similar. Not a hunt, exactly—" He pauses thoughtfully, because that's how he is about his words. "And not that I'm insinuating anything about you and Ms. Fonseca, to be clear. But we would leave each other love notes, tucked in the hole made by a rather large knot in that very tree. If you stand, you will see the tree's trunk splits and its limbs bow out, making this shape. . . ." He demonstrates with his hands. "And especially in the fall, when the leaves turn red and orange and pink—well, my oh my, Lukas, if that dang tree doesn't look just like an enormous leafy heart."

"And the whale's eye?" I ask, not that I care, necessarily. I mean, not really. Because the hunt is pretty much set in my head, and it took me a while to think of the clues, and I already know where the rest of them are supposed to go. On the other hand, I do have a pen and a small spiral pad, if I really want to redo things. And it's hard to resist what Mr. Carter is telling me. If not for the next clue, then for the one that will send Joy back home.

". . . the knot," he's saying. "Right below where the split begins. And the way the bark around it bulges out above and below it, well, it creates a big old wrinkly lid. It's nearly impossible not to see Moby Dick."

"Moby who?" I ask, my eyes getting big with surprise.

Mr. Carter laughs. "Moby Dick. From the Melville story. He's a very famous literary whale."

"Oh right," I say, even though I still don't know.

We fish for a few more minutes, but I don't catch anything, either. "Well, Lukas, I should get going now," Mr. Carter says.

I walk Mr. Carter halfway back to B&B's but then stop, explaining I should probably get on with the hiding of the clues.

"Indeed you should," he says. "Ms. Fonseca is lucky to have you as her friend."

"I was super-glad to see you, Mr. Carter," I say.

He puts a hand on my shoulder and holds my gaze. "Sure thing. Me too. It was a pleasure to have this time with you, son."

"Thanks again," I call as I start to walk away.

The sun is high in the sky, a tighter, smaller ball of burning light. The air has cooled down a bit. It must be later than I think it is.

"Mr. Brunetti?"

I turn, surprised to see Mr. Carter still standing where I left him. I take a few steps back.

"Yeah?"

"Don't ever be afraid to follow your heart."

9

JOY

MY SISTER SWINGS DAD'S TRUCK INTO THE LOT BEHIND Greer's Diner. The tires grind over the gravel; she steps on the clutch, flips the shifter into park, and shuts the engine. Most of me just wants to go home, crawl into bed, and feel sorry for myself. But Natalia seems to be ignoring that.

"Don't we have to get back?" I slump down in the seat. I was hungry an hour or two ago, but that feeling passed. "Aren't Mom and Dad mad at me?"

"I talked to them. I told them they had to lay off a bit. That you were fine, you just had some stuff you had to take care of."

"Oh yeah, what stuff? What are you talking about?" I ask innocently.

Natalia and I both sit, facing forward, not looking at each other, but totally connected. That's how it's always been with my older sister. We can go weeks without saying much more than "When are you going to get out of the bathroom?"

But neither one of us is ever that far away.

I turn and look out the passenger-side window at a huge hill of dirt. At the top, trees are clinging for their lives. Just beyond that, the woods and the bus shelter. No, not the bus shelter. I must have that wrong.

It's not right here, is it, Lukas?

"Isn't that your friend Audrey, from school?" Natalia taps on the window.

"Yeah, that's her." I'm watching Audrey and her mom coming out of the diner, each of them holding their leftovers in Styrofoam containers, but their car is parked closer to the entrance, so she won't see me unless I get out and wave or something, which I don't feel like doing.

"Didn't you used to play with her a lot?" Natalia asks.

"Play with her? I'm not six, Natty."

We both watch as Audrey's mom nearly drops her leftovers getting out her keys, but she deftly manages to unlock the car, and they both get in.

"I didn't mean it that way. I'm just saying, you guys just used to hang out more, I remember." Natalia puts her two hands back on the steering wheel and sighs. "Look, about Lukas, I know what you're doing," she says.

We *did* used to hang out more. Audrey's car backs up and swings out of the parking lot. But, wait, Natalia couldn't, she couldn't know *everything*. She might know that Lukas and I did scavenger hunts on our birthdays, but she couldn't know where I had been today or where I was going. Even I didn't know that.

Unless she opened the envelope, the one Lukas slid under our front door, a year ago today. Unless she had read it!

"And, *no*, I didn't read your note from Lukas, if that's what you're thinking. But I did see it. I'm the one that put it in your room, dodo bird."

Natalia put the letter, the first clue, in my room?

Of course, how else could it have gotten there?

It kind of makes sense. That morning, the police rang our bell. They came inside. They told us what they told us. They asked my parents some questions. They asked me some things, of which I have absolutely no memory whatsoever. I don't remember what the officers looked like or how many of them there were. Or if they were policemen or policewomen. Everything in my brain goes quiet after that, blank.

I never thought to wonder how Lukas's note got into my room, onto my desk. My name on it. In his handwriting. The envelope I didn't open. I stuffed it in my bottom drawer and never looked at it again.

Until this morning, of course.

My sister found it that morning, didn't she? Natalia was the one who put it in my room.

"Where?" I ask.

"It was under our front door. I didn't want it to get all trampled on, with all the . . . you know, people walking in and out."

"Thanks." I slouch down in the seat, pressing my knees against the glove compartment.

"I never opened it," my sister tells me. "But I knew you would one day, when you were ready. So, yeah, nothing gets by me."

"Not everything," I say softly. "You don't know how I scared him away."

"Who?" Natalia asks me.

The smell of hamburgers wafts across the parking lot and into the truck's open windows; my stomach rumbles.

"Lukas," I answer my sister.

Now I am remembering a little: it was a woman. A woman police officer, and I remember what the policewoman asked me. She was nice. She had long blond hair in a ponytail, like you wouldn't think for a police person.

She sat down on the couch next to me and talked softly. "Do you recall the last time you two spoke?"

Of course, I knew. I would never forget. It had been just the night before my birthday. On the phone. I invited him over for breakfast, like I do every year, and every year he says, "No thanks. Cake is enough celebrating for me."

It was hard for him to be around my family sometimes. There were so many of us. Davy and Isabel never left him alone, grabbing on to his legs and begging him to pick them up, toss them around, walk with their feet on top of his. I knew he worried about leftover feelings from when Natalia held on to stuff she'd heard about Lukas's brother. I get it; stories can stick to people, especially bad ones, like pancake syrup on the kitchen counter.

But he didn't need to be worried. Once they got to know him, my whole family loved him.

"Lukas is *not* his brother," I'd tell Natalia when we were alone.

I knew *that* was true, but I didn't really know anything about Justin because I never spent any time at their house. And not just because my parents were so overprotective, but I don't think Lukas wanted me there. He didn't like his mom's boyfriend, Rand, and he never knew what stupid thing his brother was going to do.

Lukas was always trying to protect me.

And I scared him away.

"You could never have scared Lukas away," Natalia tells me.

"But I did," I say. "I may have told him I loved him."

Natalia doesn't turn to look at me exactly, but I can feel her whole body shift. She's actually trying *not* to look at me, like she knows I might stop talking if she does.

But I want to talk. I've never told anyone what happened.

"It's not what I was trying to say," I begin. "I was trying to say something else."

"Like what?"

"Like, when he said he didn't want to come to breakfast, I was going to say something like, 'Well, okay, but you know I'd love you to come.'"

"But that's not how it came out. . . ."

"No."

If I stare really hard at that hill of dirt over there, it gets all blurry, until I can't make out a tree from a rock from what is nothing more than a big sheet of Plexiglas-surrounded metal.

I remember sitting with you there that day. The rain.

The story you told me.

Natalia leans back against the headrest. "And what's wrong with that?"

"He didn't *like* me like that, Natty. Not that way. I mean, we were best friends. Friends. That's all."

The best thing about my sister is that she's not my mom. Or my dad. She's not going to try and talk me out of how I feel. Or tell me I'm wrong.

She just listens.

I go on. "It was probably so embarrassing for him, too. I don't even know if he really heard me. Maybe he didn't, because he didn't say anything back. But you know Lukas, he never does. So maybe he *did* hear me."

"Is that what you are upset about? That you told him you loved him, or that you think you did?"

Wow, well, now that I'm here, I might as well go all the way.

"No, it's not that," I say. "It's not that I'm worried if he heard what I said."

I stop a minute, because it's really the first time I'm remembering any of this so clearly. "It's like I'd be more upset if he didn't. If he *didn't* hear me. If I never got to say it . . . to him. . . . If I never got to say to him . . . to tell him I love him."

Natalia is nodding her head. "Okay, look. I say we go in and have a burger. It's already one-thirty. Then you can tell me everything that's happened?"

My stomach growls in agreement.

"Okay, fine," I say.

We both get out of the truck and slam the squeaky doors shut behind us.

"So, hey, what did *the other kind of pie* mean, anyway?" Natalia asks me as we head toward the back door into Greer's Diner. "Was it, like, pizza pie? Is that Vincent's?"

But I grind my feet to a halt in the gravel. I smack my sister in the arm.

"Hey, wait a minute," I say, hitting her again. "I thought you said you didn't look in the envelope. You did, didn't you?"

"I might have peeked," Natalia says, and she starts to run ahead, across the parking lot.

I chase after her, knowing that when we get inside and sit down, I'm going to tell her everything about the waitress at Vincent's and Thea and the Revo Rocket and how now

I'm thinking maybe Mr. Carter knows something. Maybe he knows where Lukas was heading to next. And I am going to ask my sister if we can go find him.

I'm not ready to let this go.

Not yet.

LUKAS

WHAT I'M THINKING ABOUT NOW, ON THE WAY TO THE LI-
brary after finding the whale's-eye knot in the heart-shaped
tree and planting the last clue there, is how Joy punched
me that day in the rain when I tried to tell her about Execution Rocks. It was a few weeks ago, in the bus shelter
behind Greer's.

I don't know why my brain keeps doing that, thinking
about stuff with Joy, like a movie in my head that won't
stop playing.

✳

"Cut it out, Lukas. That's not true, and you know it." Joy
punches me hard on the arm, and I laugh, but she's not
laughing. "It's not really called that, is it?"

"It is true, or I wouldn't say it. I swear. That's why they
call it that. Or at least some people say."

"Is not." She shivers, so I move closer, like maybe it will
help keep her warm, which makes my shoulder accidentally
bump hers. "And you're creeping me out," she says.

115

I move away quick but then realize she just means the story, not me, so I feel dumb, because I never used to feel so confused around Joy.

"Okay, fine, then. Go ahead and finish about the island. Otherwise, I'll just keep wondering."

I smile a little, because Joy can be like that: scared and curious, both at the same exact time.

"Okay, but only if you don't punch me again."

She nods, wrapping her arms around her chest, and shivers some more, but this time I don't try to help because it's the middle of July, so it's not like she's going to freeze to death.

The reason we're soaking wet and up in the bus shelter in the first place is because Joy has some money to burn. "Mucho babysitting!" she had texted me earlier. "Let's go to Greer's!"

"Not me," I texted back, because I've been saving all my dog-walking money for her birthday gift, but she wrote back, "It's cool. I can pay for lunch."

Then, a block from Greer's, the sky had turned black and the clouds had opened up, raining down on us like Niagara Falls. Which is when I remembered the bus shelter that Justin and his friends helped the seniors move from near the school to up here as part of some senior prank this past spring.

"Up behind Greer's, can you believe it?" He had come

home at, like, four in the morning, waking me up, laughing and bragging about carting it up the hillside in the middle of the night. "You shoulda seen it, Lukulele. All the way up that hill. It was freaking hilarious."

He was talking like that, all loud and crazy, making up dumb nicknames for me on the spot, which probably meant he'd been drinking, so I was worried he was going to wake Mom. And now that Rand was gone, she was back to getting no rest, working all kinds of double shifts.

"So, anyway," I tell Joy, "at least that's the way Dad told Justin the story about the island, and later Justin told it to me." I lean out of the shelter to grab a stick that's poking from some leaves and use it like a pointer to draw a pretend map on the Plexiglas window in front of us. "There are a whole bunch of little islands out there, but most of them are just green, no buildings or anything, and impossible to see from shore. But this one here"—I tap with the stick for emphasis—"is the one with the white lighthouse. If you look hard and squint, you can see it out there."

"Execution Rocks." Joy rolls her eyes a little, like she doesn't believe me about the whole name thing.

"Right. Which is called that because they used to bring prisoners there to die."

"By execution," she says, shuddering a little.

"Well, yeah. But not exactly. What they'd do is tie them to the rocks at low tide. And when the water would come in—voilà!—no more prisoners to deal with anymore." I toss the stick back out into the woods.

"Creepy and horrible," Joy says. "They really did that?" There's hope in her voice that it's not true.

"Well, probably not," I tell her. "In fact, if you google it, it says it's only called that because of the jagged rocks that surround the island that get completely submerged at high tide. So the fishermen who don't know about them can get their boats stuck if they're not careful navigating out there."

"That still sounds pretty dangerous," Joy says.

"I guess. If you're stupid and don't know what you're doing. And you don't pay attention to the tides."

"But you do?"

"Yeah, of course. I even have a tide chart on my phone." I pat my pocket. "And if you don't believe me, they give tours there. And you can rent the lighthouse for a sleepover. So there are boats going to and from that island all the time."

"Really?"

"Yeah, sure."

"Okay, then." She leans her head against my shoulder, and my heart starts pounding so loud, I'm sure she's going to hear it in the quiet.

Quiet.

The rain has stopped. My hands are sweating.

"We should probably go to Greer's now," I say, fast.

"Yes, okay, sure."

She gets up, and we both start walking, but all the way to Greer's, I can still feel the warm spot where her head was just resting on my shoulder.

10

JOY

MR. CARTER DOESN'T LOOK AT ALL SURPRISED TO SEE ME
and Natalia standing on his front porch, but that's just how
Mr. Carter is. He's one of those teachers who really like
kids and teaching, and he remembers all his students, even
ones from ten years ago. Like my sister.

"Natalia Fonseca?"

"Yup, it's me, Mr. Carter."

"And Joy?"

I nod.

When I told Natalia my plan, when I told her about
the man in the white T-shirt and what he said about seeing Lukas outside his shop, she told me she knew where
Mr. Carter lives. She'd been there trick-or-treating once.
He had the best candy.

And if there was nothing to find out there, she said, we
would find that out together.

We. She said *we.*

Maybe Mr. Carter could tell us something, my sister

said. And then she used one of our mom's favorite expressions: "What's the worst that could happen?"

I wanted to tell her there were plenty of worse things that could happen, but I couldn't think of any.

So here we are.

He shakes both of our hands, of course. "Would you girls like to come inside? My wife would love to see you two." He smiles and adds, "Too."

When Lukas and I were in Mr. Carter's class together but before we were even friends, we waited at the same bus stop because we both lived at the Dolphin Garden Apartments. I don't think Lukas spoke to me once that whole year. Now, as I stand here on Mr. Carter's front porch, hearing his deep, familiar voice, a vivid memory forms in my head. It's of the first time I really *saw* Lukas.

He's standing at the front of the class, right between Mr. Carter's desk and the American flag. Maybe he's supposed to recite a poem or give a book report. Or maybe he's leading us in the pledge. But whatever it is, Lukas is frozen.

I was sitting in the front of the room, because, well, I always sat in the front row if I could, and I remember seeing Lukas's face, his eyes blinking back tears.

And I remember thinking he looked like he was the most alone person in the whole world.

"Joy?" Natalia is talking to me, and by the way she's saying my name, it must be the second time. Third. "Joy? Do you want to go in?"

"Oh sure."

Inside, Mrs. Carter offers us iced tea, and though we just ate at the diner, it seems rude not to accept. Mr. Carter shows us around. "It's a historic house," he tells us. Everything he renovates has to be approved by the Port Bennington Historic Society, even the doorknobs and the shelves in the pantry, and you can tell by the way he's talking, he's really proud of it.

"He does all the work himself," Mrs. Carter says, handing us each a tall glass, clinking with ice.

When we all sit down in the living room, Mr. Carter asks, "So what can I do for you girls?"

Natalia looks at me.

Wait, you're right, Lukas. Now that I hear Mr. Carter's voice, I remember.

It was a poetry recital, just like I thought.

Mr. Carter wanted us to be able to speak in front of people, clearly, slowly, and with intent. We got to dress up, if we wanted. I had memorized a poem about springtime or flowers or birds or something, and I wore my mother's butterfly scarf. Lukas wore baggy suit pants that must have once been his brother's and a too-long tie, loose around his neck, and he held up a giant, homemade, fake dollar bill.

I don't remember if Mr. Carter fed Lukas his first line, or if all of a sudden it just came to him. But now it comes to me like a punch in the stomach.

It was something about money. About a dollar bill.

And about being a son.

And some math. Like two is more than one.

It was a Shel Silverstein poem, and I thought it was so funny, I went home and I read it again and again. At least, I thought that was why I did that.

I feel my eyes stinging with tears.

"It's okay, Joy." Mrs. Carter comes and sits down next to me. She puts her hand on my back and gives me a little rub. "What can we do for you, sweetheart?" she encourages me.

I start. "Well, I was wondering if you could tell me anything about Lukas. The man at B&B's told me he saw you guys fishing . . . that day. . . . And I thought maybe you knew where Lukas was going next. I mean, what he was doing. Or, I mean, anything. I thought maybe you could tell me something."

"About the scavenger hunt? About our tree?" Mr. Carter looks over at Mrs. Carter.

He knows?

You told him.

"About the whale's eye? I think I can," Mr. Carter says.

Mrs. Carter interrupts, as if she can see the excitement

in my face and she doesn't want me to get my hopes up. "But, of course, we don't know if that's where Lukas went. We don't know at all. But I'm sure Paul can tell you a story, if you girls have a little time. . . ."

I look at Natalia, who nods.

Yes, we have time.

 # LUKAS

THINKING ABOUT JOY AND THE ISLANDS MAKES ME THINK about the night the three of us did the puzzle with Rand.

✳

"Your grandpa loved to fish, too. That's how your father knew all the names of all those little islands in the Sound," Mom says, tapping the picture on the box of the puzzle we're doing. "I bet he fished here, too."

"Dad?" I ask, confused.

"No, your grandpa Antonio," she says. "Before they moved to the States."

The puzzle is of a place in Italy called Cinque Terre, which is what makes Mom think about Grandpa Tony, I guess. I never met him. He died young like Dad did, only not from cancer, but a heart attack. Not even Justin knew him. Still, Mom likes to talk about him, and there are pictures of Grandpa Tony and Grandma Vivi and Dad, and all our other relatives, on the wall that goes down the hallway

125

from the living room. In one of them, Dad is young, and he and Grandpa Tony are standing in a boat, each holding up a beautiful silver striped bass.

One time, I caught Rand looking at the photos in the hall. Just standing there, staring at them, so I went over and stood and stared with him. After a while, he said, "You guys are lucky you have such nice stories about your dad and your grandparents and your cousins. All of my memories are [curse word]. Things and people I'd rather forget. Until you all, that is. I wish I was better at showing that."

He's showing it fine now, on this Friday night, when we're doing the puzzle of Cinque Terre. He's not out at a pub, drinking and hanging with his pals. Instead, he's here with all of us.

"I love the way it sounds—*Chinqua Terre*," Mom says, repeating it with a *ch* sound. "It means 'Island of Five Lands' or something like that."

Rand and me both repeat it now, too, using the *ch* sound, plus rolling our *r*'s, all exaggerated like Mom did.

On the box lid, colorful houses of red, yellow, and blue are all stacked together on this super-high cliffside as if they're about to slide down into the deep blue sea.

"We'll go there on our honeymoon, how about it, Mel?" Rand asks, waggling his eyebrows at Mom. She rolls her eyes at him, but she smiles also. I think she's happy this month, because Rand has been working hard to go to meetings and not lie about bars or drinking beers. He really does want to marry her, I think. Though this is the first time I've heard him say it.

I look over at Justin to see if he heard, and his gaze shifts to me. He's lying on the couch, playing a game on his phone, because he's already in high school, and way too cool to do puzzles with us.

"Pine Island. Neptune Island. Pea Island," he says, so it's clear he's paying attention. He sits up and continues to count off names on his fingers. "Captain's. David's." He's naming the islands Dad taught him, though I'm not sure why. It's like even when Rand is trying, Justin has to remind him about all the stuff our real father did. "Schultz's. And Execution Rocks, where the lighthouse is."

I count them off in my head, too, but not out loud. I can't help myself. Lots of people don't even know those islands exist, right close to where we live.

"Tell me again, will you?" Rand says, standing up to stretch, then surprising me by walking over and sitting down on the couch right next to where Justin is. He pats Justin's knee. "Seems I always forget one or two of them."

"Not in the mood," Justin says, going back to his game, but Rand stays there, anyway, because he gives Justin a lot of room to be mad at him for no reason at all.

✳

The memory goes from happy to sad as I'm thinking about how Rand was trying and Justin had to give him a hard time. Then again, Rand started drinking again right after that, like so many times, so I guess Justin was right not to trust him.

I pass by Greer's, happy to turn the corner to the library and not to think about Justin or Rand, or even me and Joy, right now and just focus on the hunt instead.

Clue #6 is already rewritten and inside the tree. So, only Clue #5, which I'll hide in the library, needs to be fixed so it leads her there. On the bench outside the main entrance, I sit and take out the small spiral pad and my pen.

"*Clue #5*," I write, tapping the pen to my forehead, then think, *What will get Joy to the gazebo?*

Music.

Where you hear music, I start, because she'll get that fast, except, no, maybe not, because there's also Spin Doctor's, the used-record shop, plus the fancy Port Bennington concert hall. Or maybe she'll think I just mean somebody's radio in their car, or even the music room or auditorium in our school.

So I scratch that out, turn the page, and start again:

> *By the piers, on the lawn,*
> *Near a shelter that's round,*

> *Where violins and harps*
> *Sometimes make their sounds,*

I scratch that out, too, because the rhyme is crappy, and try again:

> *By the piers on the lawn,*
> *Near a shelter that's round,*
> *Where violins and harps*
> *Make a nice summer sound,*

Better. But not enough, because I still need to get her to the tree.

I add under that:

> *Look for the leaves*
> *Of the heart-shaped tree*
> *(I know it sounds corny*
> *But it has a secret history).*

And since I'm on a total roll with this good clue now, I add:

> *Find the tree, then its knot*
> *that's the eye of a whale.*
> *Peek inside and you'll find*
> *A clue, without fail.*

It's a little longer than the other clues, but so what? Plus, it's getting later than I thought, so I don't have a ton of time to fix it. The library closes early on Saturdays.

I tear out the page, fold it into quarters, scrawl *JOY* on the front, and head into the nice, cool air-conditioning.

11

JOY

SOMETIMES OUT HERE ON LONG ISLAND, IN THE SUMMER, we get these little sun showers, which means that the sun is still shining everywhere, but all of a sudden, without warning, it's raining. It can be hard, too, like pellets hitting you on the head. Or in this case, our windshield.

Natalia flips the wipers on, and they chase each other back and forth.

"Take my phone and text Mom. No, Dad," my sister says. "Tell him we're fine; we went for lunch, and we'll be home in less than an hour." She keeps her eyes on the road and nudges her bag toward me. "It's in that little zipper part. See it?"

I dig in, feel around, find her phone, and do what she told me, but before I can finish swiping through all her new apps and sneaking a peek at her photos, her phone chimes back at me once, with a text.

"Dad," I tell Natalia.

"What's it say?"

"He says: 'OK. Drive carefully.'"

131

"Good. Leave it at that."

I am about to drop her phone back into her bag when it rings.

"Mom," I tell Natalia.

"Do not answer it," my sister says.

I start to object. "They'll worry. Maybe I should just pick up and get it over with."

"You texted, right? They know you're with me, right? You're thirteen today, aren't you?" Natalia ticks off. "If you pick up the phone, Mom will guilt you into coming home. We won't find this tree today, and we might not ever know if there's something there for you."

We wait for the ringing to stop and then for the inevitable beep of a voicemail.

"I'll take all the blame," my sister says. "I promise."

I believe her. She'll either take the blame, or they'll be happy enough to dump it on her. That's how it usually goes. It's nobody's fault, really. It's just the way things are. She's the oldest. She does everything first, and she gets in trouble for it first. Not to mention they've been tiptoeing around me all year. I figure by the time they get to Isabel and Davy, there won't be any rules left at all.

The rain is already stopping, and now the wetness is like crystals that have fallen from the sky and glimmer on every surface. The gazebo that Mr. Carter told us about is on the other end of town, all the way back near the bait-and-tackle shop. It would seem I've crisscrossed almost all of Port Ben-nington in just over three and a half hours.

It's almost three o'clock.

I don't think I've been on my own, unaccounted for, that long before in my whole life. But it feels good. Kind of like being let out after being hidden away—even if I did the hiding myself—like the sky clearing, and the air smells so fresh.

"This is rainbow weather, you know?" I say, looking out the window and up at the blue breaking through. "After a rain like that. With the sun shining."

"Do you see one?"

I twist my neck and try to look way up. "Nope. Too many buildings."

"Let's take Beach Road, then. It's a little longer but it's still the right direction." Natalia cuts the wheel, makes a sharp left, and my nose bangs against the glass.

"Ouch."

"That's the spirit."

LUKAS

I STAY LONGER IN THE LIBRARY THAN I MEAN TO, BECAUSE *Love That Dog* isn't on the shelf, so I panic, thinking it's checked out, which would screw everything up, since that's where I *need* to put this next clue. Since that's where the clue I stashed under the Revo Rocket reel sends Joy to. Once she reads it, she'll know exactly where to look, and nothing else but inside that book will work:

> So much depends
> Upon a dumb blue car.
> Too bad I made you
> Walk so far. ☺

That was my easiest clue, and also I laughed out loud writing it, because *Love That Dog* is both of our favorite book. Joy's because she likes poems, and mine because I like dogs, and also it's short.

We read it at the same time in fourth grade, even though we weren't in class together, because our teachers opened the dividing wall between our classrooms for literature circles, and Joy and me got into the same circle. Ever since then, whenever we're trying to decide on something and one of us says, "It depends," the other will automatically ask, "On a blue car or a red wheelbarrow?" without even thinking about it.

It comes from the part in the book where the main character, Jack, has to write a poem and writes, *So much depends upon a blue car*, which comes from a famous poem about a red wheelbarrow.

Me: What are you getting for lunch today? Mac 'n' cheese or a hamburger?

Joy: It depends.

Me: On a blue car or a red wheelbarrow?

Joy: Do you want to watch a movie at my house tonight?

Me: It depends on which movie. And whether Izzie will be choosing it.

Joy: And on a blue car or a red wheelbarrow.

Anyway, it turned out the book wasn't checked out or missing or anything, just on display in the poetry section, but I had to ask the librarian, who figured it out. Then, when she got it down for me, she tried to walk me to the circulation desk to check it out. So I had to pretend I wanted to read it right then and there, and then she just watched me for, like, practically fifteen minutes while I sat in the kids' section and pretended. But then I got lucky because she went on break, so I quick-slipped the book in its original alphabetical-by-author place on the shelf.

Now, as I head outside into daylight, the sun is still high in the sky, but something has shifted so you can tell it's later, like the sun is working hard to hold on to the afternoon.

I weave my way down the wheelchair ramp, wishing I had my skateboard and thinking of all the days Justin and me used to zoom down this ramp and around the empty parking lot, back when he would still do stuff with me.

Halfway down the ramp, my brain stops thinking about that, because a short way down the hill by the basketball courts, I can hear laughing and voices, and one of them I recognize. Justin, with his friends, the ones he's not supposed to hang around with.

Chance isn't with him, and if they went to the Point, no way they'd be back here already.

I move closer and squat down behind a car and watch. They're drinking, clear as day. Justin takes a long sip from a bottle and tosses it into the trees.

"Hey, Brunetti, you want a hit?" one of the guys says, holding something up, then walks over to him. My chest squeezes. I don't need to stick around to see.

I stand up to walk away, and someone yells for me— "Hey, Lukas! Lukas, wait!"—but I don't stop, don't look back, not to answer or see my brother, hand shielding his eyes, squinting in my direction.

136

12

JOY

THE SUDDEN RAINSTORM HAD SENT EVERYBODY RUSHING to gather their blankets and towels and umbrellas, their portable baby cabanas, their rolling fifteen-gallon coolers, and running to their SUVs and back to their summer houses. It's a little damp, but now this whole stretch of beach is empty. Natalia and I have been waiting so long to see if a rainbow will appear in the sky that we've almost forgotten why we are lying here in the sand, with our hands folded behind our heads, looking up at the clouds.

"My butt is getting wet," I say.

"I told you to grab a sweatshirt from the back of the truck to sit on."

I stare up at the sky again. It's blue, all blue.

"So, what if there's no note in the tree?" I ask. "Hey, does that look like a dragon to you?" I point straight up, almost directly overhead.

"Why does everyone see dragons and bunny rabbits in the clouds?" my sister says. "No one ever says they see a chain saw, do they? Or a bar of soap. Or a toothbrush. And so what if it's not there?"

"What?"

"The tree. The note," Natalia says.

I think about that for a minute. It feels good to just be lying here, side by side. I can actually think and breathe.

It all happened so fast today. It's almost like a year has gone by, flying up in front of my face. I think I need to slow down and just lie here for a while. Like one of those giant stop signs in the cartoons just showed up right in front of my face and said stop.

Pause.

Slow down.

Breathe.

"Well, if it's not there, then that's the end of that," I say.

As soon as I hear my own words, I feel the familiar tugging at the corners of my mouth and the burn in my throat. Then it sticks right in the center of my chest, like a giant fist, squeezing and squeezing. It couldn't hurt more if someone had taken a Wiffle ball bat and walloped me in the gut with it, which actually happened to me once in PE, by accident, so I know.

I feel my sister take my hand and loop her fingers in between mine, and the tightness in my heart eases up.

"Look up there," she says. "It feels like we are moving, doesn't it?"

I follow the tip of her purple nail polish into the air, to a gathering of white clouds off to our left, which are forming and re-forming across the sky.

"Well, we are."

"I know, but isn't that weird, how we can see it?"

"It's not really weird. The earth is rotating east, slower than the clouds, which are being moved by the jet stream, also moving west to east, except in the Southern Hemisphere, where they would be . . ."

I'm too tired to talk anymore.

"They would be what?" Natalia sits up next to me. "They would be what, Joy?"

I'm really tired, like I've got a blanket of rocks over me.

My sister pokes me. "I'm interested. I am. Tell me. They would be *what?*"

I keep the back of my head resting in the perfect little head indent I've made in the sand. I stare up at the sky, at the light scattering in the way that makes it look yellow, later orange, then red, then deep scarlet. Lukas would know the wavelengths. He'd know the formula, the speed of light, the way sounds travel over the surface of water, how to use a compass and protractor and a nautical slide rule and everything else it takes to navigate in the open water.

How did you let this happen, Lukas?

How could you do this to me?

To you?

The sun is already edging toward the west, toward the

end of today. It is almost the end of summer. I know this feeling so well, the way the sky looks, the way the air smells, the way the coolness slides in, along with the wide shadow that creeps across the sand, turning it from white to gray.

And when today is over, the earth will have turned another 366 times; 365 days will have passed. My birthday will be over, and it will be that much closer to Lukas's, which he will never have.

"I miss him, Natty."

"I know you do."

I am so grateful she doesn't say: "We all do." So I go on. "Sometimes it hurts so much, I don't know what to do."

With that, Natalia plants her hands and hops up to her feet in one graceful motion. "Get up. Let's get going. Let's go find that tree." She reaches her hand down to me.

"And if there's nothing there?" I ask again, lifting myself up against her weight.

"Then there's nothing there. And it won't mean anything more than that. But who knows, maybe it's the looking more than the finding."

Now that the sun is out again, people are starting to file back onto the beach. A mom and her three kids, and somehow she is holding hands with all of them. A man and his son kicking a soccer ball back and forth. Two kids with a giant blow-up swan are running toward the water. It's okay to be happy.

There's still a good deal of daylight left.

LUKAS

THE THING ABOUT MORNING IS EVERYTHING FEELS LIGHTER and more hopeful. Mom used to tell me that when I couldn't sleep. When I would toss and turn because I could hear Justin awake, late, in his own room.

He couldn't sleep, so I couldn't sleep.

Back when he used to take care of me.

Not like last night, when neither of us were talking to each other.

I made mac 'n' cheese when I got home, and purposely didn't leave any for him, like I normally do. Then I left Mom a note saying, *Good night, I love you,* and went to my room.

Before I fell asleep, Joy called, like always. To talk and make plans for today.

"The clue will be there early. You just need to find it," I said. "Be prepared."

I heard the soft whistle of her breath, the squeak of her bed as she changed position. "Okay, I will," she said.

We were quiet for a minute, then I blurted, "Justin lied to me. Said he was fishing, when he wasn't."

"Really? Why? What was he doing?"

I swallowed back the sad feeling in my throat and picked the most direct words. "Drinking beers and smoking weed behind the library."

"Ouch," she said. "I'm sorry. Are you gonna tell your mom?"

"I don't know."

Joy didn't judge me, or tell me what to do. "Natalia tells me some of her friends sometimes do stuff, but that doesn't mean they're all bad. He'll come around, Lukas," was all she said.

"I know." I swallowed the upset feelings and let the thought that she was right settle into my bones. I wanted to believe her. Justin would come around. He wasn't as bad as those other kids. He wasn't like Rand.

"Lukas?"

"Yeah?"

"Come to breakfast in the morning. Everyone wants you to."

"I'll come for cake later, like I always do."

"You should do both. They all said so. Mom, Dad, Izzie, Natalia. Davy. Everyone."

"That is everyone—and a lie, because Davy barely talks." She laughed, and I smiled. "Anyway, no thanks, Joy. Night."

"Okay. I love you."

"Wait. Huh?" I asked, but she was gone.

I hung up, too, and stared at my phone, but it couldn't have been right, what I heard. It was only my tired brain playing tricks on me.

Probably what she said was *Okay, but I'd love you to* about breakfast, and my dumb ears were hearing things.

But what if?

My eyes go to the box on my desk that holds the heart necklace. *What if Joy also loves me loves me, too?*

Either way, this morning, I'm feeling surer. I will leave her the note with the gift. Even if the thought of it makes my hands sweat.

I roll over and glance out the lower part of my window, out the long, thin rectangle of glass where the shade isn't pulled down all the way. Our apartment is quiet. Justin is still sleeping, and since it's Sunday, Mom gets to sleep in, too.

Outside, I can see a section of the tree trunks of the row of silver poplars they planted all around this place when they built it, their white bark slashed by deep gray lines. They look like the tall necks of albino giraffes marching outside my window, on parade.

And suddenly I remember this game Mom used to play with Justin and me when we were little, called Head, Bodies, Feet. I haven't thought about that in the longest time. We'd play lots of word games and puzzle games when we

143

were stuck in the hospital waiting room, while Dad was having his treatments and surgeries. I don't remember all of them, but I remember this one now.

Each of us got a piece of paper and had to draw a head on the top. It could be any kind of head: a boy's; a girl's; an old lady's, with glasses and a pointy nose; a guy's, with a crazy handlebar mustache and lunatic beard. Whatever came into your brain.

Then we'd each fold the paper down at the top, so only the bottom of the neck was sticking out, and pass it to the person on our right. That person would draw a body, then fold it down, with only the top of the legs showing, and pass it again, and the last person would add the rest of the legs and feet. At the end, we'd each open our complete drawing to see what kind of head was on what kind of body with what kind of feet.

And there was one where Justin drew the head, and I got the body, and Mom got the legs and feet, and when we opened it, Justin had drawn a giraffe's head with a long orange neck, and I had put a dress on it, though you could barely tell what it was. And Mom had given it clown shoes. And in the middle of the waiting room, we all started laughing like crazy. Mom was crying, she was laughing so hard. And there we were, all three of us, laughing our heads off, even though Dad was dying. And when we finished laughing, Mom turned to us, maybe more to Justin than to me, and she touched his cheek and said, "I promise everything is going to be okay."

I roll onto my back and stare at the ceiling for a while, thinking about how most people hate to get up early, and a lot of times I do, too, but not when I'm going fishing, and not today because it's Joy's birthday.

I stretch and yawn, and even though I'm excited, for a split second I do think about hitting snooze, going back to sleep for eight more minutes. I don't need to get to her house this early. But I'm awake now, so might as well. I need to hide the box, with the note and the heart pendant, too, and the earlier I get it there, the earlier she'll find the first clue. For sure, she'll figure out it means Vincent's Pizza, and that this hunt is bigger and better than any of our other hunts before. And that will build up the excitement so she can hardly stand it while she's finishing breakfast and waiting for her family to set her free.

13

JOY

AS WE DRIVE OVER THE BAY BRIDGE TOWARD THE PARK THAT Mr. Carter told us about, I can't stop my whole body from feeling the anticipation, no matter how many times my logical brain is telling it not to.

I'm okay.

Just like Natalia said, it's not like anything will change.

The note will be there. Or it won't.

But something else is pulling at me, knocking around in my insides, starting out like a whisper, like a song I sang all the time, but now I forget the words.

Remember?

Do you remember those times I was happy?

I do.

There is a perfectly square patch of lawn in the center of our apartment complex; it felt huge to us, with Lukas's building—tall and imposing—on one side, mine on the other. There is just grass, surrounded by a low metal fence, like the scalloped collar of a dress. And a sign.

NO DOGS.

"It doesn't say, 'no kids,'" Lukas declared.

And so that's where we planted our candy garden. I don't think we really believed we were going to grow candy, but it's not that we *didn't* believe it. It was more like that kind of in-between, magical kid thinking, when it didn't matter either way.

First we used Skittles.

I was nine, and two days older, and I had the authority. "You dig the hole, and I'll drop them in."

Red and blue and green were staining my hands. I dropped one into each little spot that Lukas uncovered, and I watched while he carefully brushed the mound of dirt back over the top and smoothed it all down.

I don't know how long we had our candy garden. A few weeks that spring? I think we planted some Sour Patch and some gummy worms. Every day we came out and watered them, long after the candy had been washed away or been eaten by the squirrels.

Remember that day when we ran for our lives?

Remember when the super saw us digging in there and started yelling?

"Hey, you kids, get off the grass. Whaddaya think you're doing?"

"Ruuun!" Lukas shouted. "Run."

We leapt over the little metal fence, and we ran as fast as we could. We ran past the courtyard, out of the back gate, and down the path, past the elementary school. We ran all the way to the seawall, till there was nowhere else to run.

We ran to the end of the world.

"Oh man. Do you think Mr. Sweeny followed us?" Lukas asked, plopping himself down on the stone wall, and me right next to him.

We were out of breath and panting, and so excited that our toes and our ears were tingling. The stone wall was damp and cold, the ocean was spread out before us and blended into the blue sky above. The sun was new and belonged only to us.

I looked around in all possible directions, like a sentinel on guard, but there was no way Mr. Sweeny would have followed us this far. "No sign of him," I reported.

You smiled a happy smile at me.

"That was a close call," Lukas said.

"Whew."

"Whew."

"I've never run so fast in my whole life," I said.

My chest hurt so good. My legs were shaking. I don't think I'd ever been that happy.

 LUKAS

I HEAD RIGHT INTO THE SHOWER, CAREFUL TO BE QUIET AND not wake anyone. As the water streams down, I think about Dad, not that I can remember a lot. It's always more like a feeling of him, from what Justin and Mom say, than my own real memories.

But I know Mom loved him for a long time. And that he loved her, and didn't want to leave us at all.

I also think about how happy Mom seemed when she started dating Rand, because she had someone who helped her, and someone she liked to spend time with.

I think about Rand, too, and how excited we all were when he moved in. And how it took a while for Mom to say okay, he could, because she was looking out for us instead of her.

And when we first started seeing how much he would drink, it didn't seem like a big deal. Not really. It was only when he started to sleep more, or lie, or get angry and mean and yell.

And then Mom was always saying sorry to us, like it was her fault Rand drank, not his.

"Sorry, I thought he would stop."

"Sorry, he's trying. He wants to."

"Sorry, I think it might be better this time."

But it would only get better for a short while, and then finally it got bad enough he crashed his truck. That night, Mom cried and thanked God she got a special warning, because neither me or Justin were with him.

That was the night she did it. Told Rand he had to leave.

"Don't come back until you're sober for six months, promise me that," she'd said, and that was almost nine months ago.

And now things are getting better again. Mom doesn't cry and miss him so much. We just need to find her another person to help her feel happy.

I grab the shampoo and lather up, and since I don't want to think about all that anymore, I make the water hotter, turn my face into the stream, and think about the silver poplars instead. I know it's weird how I pay attention to them, but I like to pay attention to the things around me, like fish and water and clouds. Like islands and trees. Joy says it's one of the things she likes best about me.

And I'm thinking about how a lot of people around here complain about them, because they cause allergies and send saplings out like alien spawn, and so every spring, Mr. Sweeny slips a survey under our doors, asking if they should all be cut down and replaced.

You'd think it was a good thing, to have a lot of trees. But I guess some things can be good *and* bad at the same time. Some people just want grass and flowers more than they want to live in a forest of silvery trees.

On the way back to my room, I pass Justin's room and can hear him snoring away like a lawn mower.

I backtrack and push open his door a little to look at him. It won't matter, because even a bomb won't wake my brother. It makes me happy to see him there, sleeping, because those bad kids stay out all night and he doesn't, and even though he's seventeen, when he's asleep like that, it reminds me he's still just a peaceful kid.

I think how it must be lots of pressure on him, about to be a senior and not knowing whether he wants to go to college or not, not knowing what he'll do after. So, maybe it's understandable if he needs to blow off a little steam.

And then I remember how when Rand left, Justin promised me he'd never be like him, only like our dad, because even though Dad's gone, he knows he still needs to make him proud.

"Not that he can see us, exactly," Justin said, "but I believe he can, sort of. Not with his eyes, but with something else." He punched his fist to his chest then and rumpled my hair. "And he knows that we'll both be okay."

I had only nodded because my words were pressed down by my tears.

"And that we'll always take care of Mom," he had added.

I had nodded, for sure, at that, too.

14

JOY

WE ARE HEADING ACROSS THE GRASS BY THE GAZEBO, where they have concerts in the summer, and we both stop when we see it, the only tree looming out so majestically from the manicured lawn.

Natalia gives me a push. "Go on," she says.

It's a real push, with her hands on my back. I stumble a little, but I start walking, focused straight ahead.

This must be the one, the right tree, the one Mr. Carter told us about. He did say the trunk splits into two limbs that are bowed out, and that there is a knot in the center, where the bark looks like a gray, wrinkled whale's eye. Like that one.

This must be the tree.

I'm sure that's how he described it, but now that I am standing here, I see something else.

Am I crazy?

I see a heart.

This whole huge tree, standing out in the middle of everywhere for everyone to see, from this distance looks like a giant heart.

153

I swear it does.

I turn around and look back, because Natalia isn't following me anymore, but she's standing there, watching, and nodding her head. When I get closer, right up to the tree, the heart disappears and I see the twisted knot, the hole in the bark.

The whale's eye.

There are holes in the dirt and holes in fences and holes that are to dig and holes you should never blindly stick your hand into. But that never seemed to stop Lukas.

✳

"I don't think this is such a good idea."

We were both squatting down, as close to the ground as we could, knees bent up to our shoulders, our bodies perfectly balanced on our feet. So we could get a better look.

It was a neatly round hole, about half a foot wide, deep in the sand, so deep we couldn't see the bottom. Lukas was poking around with a stick. I remember it was winter. The beach was cold, the sand was hard, and the wind was biting us like someone was throwing tiny stones.

"What is it?" I asked.

"I don't know. But I think there's something down there."

"Exactly," I told him.

My mom had brought us to the beach that day, but we weren't supposed to be this far down, on the other side of the seawall, the huge stone wall that keeps our whole town from falling into the sea.

Lukas dropped the stick. "I gotta just find out."

Slowly, he lowered his hand inside, past his fingers and then up to his wrist. When he couldn't reach any more, he lowered his whole body onto the sand, and his elbow disappeared, too. He stopped with half his arm still down in the hole, and he looked straight at me.

"I feel something," he said.

"Be careful," I told him.

"For sure, there's something down here."

I couldn't much contain my fear, and my excitement. I didn't offer much help, besides repeating, "Be careful. What is it? What is it? Be careful" over and over.

What grade were we in?

Fourth?

Fifth?

Then suddenly Lukas's face contorted and twisted. His eyes popped open, then his mouth, and he let out a strangled yelp. With his arm still halfway down into the sand, his body began dancing around, his legs kicking out under him.

I didn't hesitate. I grabbed on to his other arm, digging my fingers into the material of his jacket, around the skinny bones of his arm, and I heaved myself backward with all the strength I could muster. I pulled and I pulled.

And we both went flying backward. My hat blew off and sailed down the beach.

I never did find that hat again, you know.

We landed on our butts in the cold, wet sand, but Lukas was safe. I had managed to yank his arm out of the hole, and away from whatever horrible thing had caught on to him. I had saved him.

But when I looked up, he was doubled over, laughing. Oh, he was so pleased with himself.

"I hate you," I yelled at him. Just to make my point. "I'll never forgive you." I headed for the stone steps leading back up to our apartment.

Lukas ran after me.

He was way faster.

"I'm sorry, Joy. I'm really sorry," he said, the happiness still plastered all over his face. "But c'mon. It was a good one, right? You have to admit."

Yeah, it was a good one. A doozy.

I am smiling now, just thinking about it, even thinking about it in past tense.

Maybe this tree is a heart and this bark is an eye, but there's definitely a hole, a deep hole in this trunk, and if there ever was something in here, it would have been kept dry and safe, way down deep.

I have to reach really far inside, and it's hard to touch, but I know I have to.

I know it's time.

LUKAS

THERE ARE MOMENTS THAT CHANGE EVERYTHING. LIKE THE moment with Joy at the front of Mr. Carter's room in second grade, when our school birthdays collided and I helped give out her tie-dye cupcakes.

Like the moment Mom and Justin and me all laughed at the giraffe-girl-clown, even though Dad was dying, which let us know, somehow, that everything would be all right.

Like Mr. Carter being at B&B's and wanting me to sit and fish with him so he could tell me about the whale's-eye tree, because before that story, I wasn't sure about the pendant or actually being brave enough to tell Joy how I feel.

But now I am.

Now I know everything I'm doing is the exact right thing.

I grab the envelope with her name, and the box wrapped in red construction paper, which holds the note and the gift, and walk quietly out of my bedroom and down the hall.

But when I get to the front door, I stop in my tracks, the breath sucked out of me. There, too, waits a small, little moment that changes everything.

15

JOY

"IT'S HERE. THE CLUE IS HERE," I WHISPER TO MYSELF.

I feel it with my fingers, and I know what it is before I even pull it out. I feel the edgy tips of the paper, the same as the three others I've found. And right on the front, before I can even open it, will be Lukas's handwriting.

Yup, that's his handwriting, all right.

You made it to the last clue!
☺

 LUKAS

TIMBERLAND BOOTS WITH THE WORD *PRO* WRITTEN ON orange tabs on the backs of them.

Boots that *clump, clump, clump*ed beside me so many times, going down to the marina to go fishing.

Sitting there by our front door.

Now, I mean.

This minute.

The thing that changes everything, sends my stomach into a knot, is a dumb pair of work boots by the door.

If they were other construction boots, maybe I wouldn't have even noticed or paid attention or cared. Maybe I'd have thought Mom brought a date home, even though she doesn't do that very often. Or maybe I would have thought one of Justin's friends crashed overnight, sacked out on the floor of his room on the far side of his bed.

But the orange PRO means one thing only.

Because Justin and me used to make fun of it.

Him.

Rand.

Wearing those PRO boots. Especially when Justin was mad at him.

"I guess he's a pro if his shoes say so," Justin would say. Then both of us would bust out laughing.

He must be here. In Mom's room. So, I'm not laughing now.

But what if he's different?

You can't believe him, Lukas, Justin had said. *He lies. Drunks lie. That's what they do.*

But Mom made him swear.

What if that's the reason he's back?

He promised.

But I'm not dumb. My brain knows better. And Justin will freak if he sees him here.

I walk to the window that looks down on the parking lot, my whole body shaking with sudden cold.

And, yeah, it's there. His motorcycle, parked next to Mom's car.

Anger rises, thick and sour in my throat.

I don't want him here. Not for her and not for us.

Not if he's going to leave us again.

Not if he's going to lie.

I don't want to be back to the place where people talk about us, about how he gets drunk and yells, and how he and Mom fight. How they can hear the fighting from outside.

But maybe he is different.

161

Maybe he's sober.

He wouldn't come back if he wasn't.

Still, my legs shake.

My breath comes in short, shallow puffs.

I need to calm down and think.

My brain changes my plans.

I was going to go to Joy's building and then come back here and wait. Wait for her to text that she's ready. Wait to meet her at Vincent's and set out on the hunt with her. But now, instead, I grab my bike and a sweatshirt from the hall closet.

I'll drop off the clue and hide the gift and then ride out to the dock near the Point.

It's still super-early. Plenty of time.

I'll head out on the *Angler* for a while.

There I can think.

There I can breathe.

Maybe I'll even make it to Execution Rocks.

That will mean something. Proof I can deal with this all.

16

JOY

I STARE AT THE PAPER.

> Clue №6

I missed two whole clues. I'll never know what they said.

Lukas, did you send me to Mr. Carter?

I wait for an answer. When I don't get one, I look down at the paper in my hands.

> *The world is a circle.*
> *This tree is a heart.*
> *↑ That very last word*
> *Leads you back to the ____.*
> *When you get there, go slow,*
> *Though you won't miss a clue,*
> *You may miss the best part*
> *I planted for you.*

I read it one more time to make sure I've got this right. Make sure I understand.

I do.

I know I do.

I know more clearly than I've known almost anything.

I turn around and shout to my sister.

 # LUKAS

I LEAVE MY BIKE OUTSIDE AND PRESS THE CODE INTO JOY'S building, and run up the two flights of stairs and down the hall to the Fonsecas' corner apartment.

The building is so quiet on a Sunday morning at this hour. Sun floods in through the two high windows at each end of the hall.

Only one person walks out into the hallway, to empty a pail down the trash chute. "Good morning," I say, like I belong here. By now most everyone in this hallway knows me, and wouldn't care either way.

At the Fonsecas' front door, my heart races, my brain skipping back to last night. Joy's voice on the phone.

Okay. I love you.

Or *Okay. I'd love you to.*

Does it really matter which one?

It could, I remind myself. Because once I do this, it's over. It's done. My feelings for Joy will be clear.

Justin's words from yesterday morning come back to me. *Nothing ruins a friendship like declaring your undying love.*

But Justin is wrong. She'll always be my friend. My best friend. And I don't need to lie, or pretend I don't feel what I feel.

I slide the envelope with Clue #1 under the door, then wedge the red box with her name, and the note folded inside, into the branches of the fake potted plant outside it.

17

JOY

ONCE UPON A TIME, THERE WAS A TREE.

And the tree was a heart.

The world is a circle.

I'm not crazy.

This tree is a heart.

Because Lukas saw it, too, and now I am holding Lukas's note in my hand, in both my hands, while we speed along Shore Road, with my sister holding fast to the steering wheel.

↑ That very last word
Leads you back to the _____.
When you get there, go slow,
Though you won't miss a clue,

You may miss the best part
I planted for you.

Well, I'm not sure what that second part is, but that first part can only mean one thing.

To head.

Home.

LUKAS

THESE ARE THE THINGS WE KEEP HIDDEN UNDER THE planks of the old, abandoned dock near the Point:

The *Angler*, deflated.

Two oars.

Three fishing rods, one of them Chance's.

The trolling motor.

Two old life vests that Mom made us promise to use whenever we go out (Chance brings his own if there are three of us).

A battery-powered tire pump that Chance gave us to keep here, which is way faster than the bicycle hand pump we had to use before.

I tap my sweatshirt pocket to be sure I remembered the extra batteries, in case. They corrode really fast out here.

I yank and pull, trying to get the *Angler* up and out of the narrow space, which is harder to do than it sounds, because when Justin is with me, he lifts the dock a little while I pull, but I can't do that alone. And, also, the last few times we came out here together, we dug the ditch deeper so no one could spot our supplies from up top, accidentally.

When I finally drag it fully out and unfold it, I'm sweating like crazy. An army of spiders and crickets and water bugs skitters away, from where they got shaken from the damp, quiet nooks and crannies of the *Angler*.

I get that feeling, needing to escape.

Needing to just get away.

18

JOY

I TAKE THE STAIRS TWO AT ONCE.

I don't have time to dig my key out of my pocket, or wait for Natalia.

I am pounding on my front door.

Anybody home? Let me in.

LUKAS

INFLATING THE *ANGLER* IS A PIECE OF CAKE.

After that, I hook the trolling motor on to the mount Rand made for it, and toss the oars in, just in case.

Overhead, the sun is trying to wake up and break out, but the clouds keep hiding it away.

I chuck one of the life vests in, too, shoving the other one, with the pump, back under the planks, and drag the *Angler* down the grassy bank toward the water.

There, I trace the edge of the far shore with my gaze, searching for the seven islands in the still-evaporating mist.

Mom would be so mad if she knew I was going out all alone.

I squint to see the lighthouse through the fog as I wade into the surf, give a last tug on the *Angler*'s rope, and jump in, using an oar to keep shoving us off, away from shore.

I need to do this.

To think.

Even Mom would understand.

It's like this poster Ms. Picone, our English teacher,

had up on her classroom wall last year. It was a picture of a rock jetty leading out to the ocean at sunrise. It said this underneath:

You can't cross the water by merely standing on shore and staring out at the sea.

So, I need to cross.
I need to go out to sea.

19

JOY

MY DAD ANSWERS THE DOOR. "WHAT IS IT? WHAT'S WRONG?"

I push past him. I feel like a tornado entering the room, not caring what or who I bump into, until I realize I have no idea what to look for.

This is my house. There's nothing here that I don't know is here.

Other than the note, the first clue that was in my drawer.

"Jolie?" My mother rushes in from the kitchen. I can smell dinner, my birthday dinner. It's always the same thing. Each one of us gets our favorite meal on our birthday, and even as we get older, we always pick the same.

Mine is mac 'n' cheese, peas, and applesauce. But my mother makes it all from scratch, with three cheeses and potato-chip topping. She even makes the applesauce.

"Are you girls all right?" she asks. Natalia is a few steps behind me.

"She's fine, Ma," Natalia says. "We just thought Lukas might have . . ." She hesitates.

I didn't want anyone to even say his name for so long.

174

I had everyone afraid to talk about him in front of me. But that wasn't right. It was exactly opposite. You *need* to talk about a person. Or they will disappear. You need to *keep* talking about them. That's how you hold on to them.

By remembering.

"I thought there might be something here for me," I interrupt. "From Lukas. Something he might have left. Something. Like a present or something?"

I look to my mother's and my father's faces.

"Nothing?" Natalia asks.

They both shake their heads.

"Come, sit down," my mother says. "Tell us what's going on. Natalia told us you girls were on a treasure hunt of some kind."

So I tell them.

"A scavenger hunt," I say. "Lukas made it for me, for my birthday. Last year. I never opened it. You knew we did that, right? All the clues. We've been doing it since we were little."

A paper-clip bracelet.

A rock painted like a polar bear.

A Shrinky Dinks key chain.

"I didn't know you were still doing it," my mother says gently. "That's so wonderful. And the clues brought you *here?*"

"Yes." I describe each clue, the first one that I had hidden in my room for a year, then the pizza place, the peacock hat, the tackle shop. Also, the man in the white T-shirt and Mr. Carter. At which point, Natalia jumps in to explain how she made sure I had lunch. Finally, the tree shaped like a heart.

And the last clue.

Exclamation point.

Smiley face.

"I don't think there could be anything here," my father says. "But it was such a terrible morning. So hectic. So sad. Unless there's something we are forgetting."

We all remember that day, and slowly we all start taking turns to talk, sharing our memories. The police. What they told us. How hard it was raining that morning. How dark it was outside. The sudden winds that had come up out of nowhere from the east. Severe thunderstorms. A series of lightning strikes reported right over the water where they had found him. They knew what had happened, the police told us as we all sat right here, exactly where we are sitting now.

# LUKAS

PAST THE MOORED BOATS, IN THE MIDDLE OF THE HARBOR, is the first time I look up again, and out toward the horizon. Before that, I was just watching the white trail of wake water. Now, out here, the islands are coming clearer through the mist.

I say their names aloud because it's good for focus:

"Pea Island.

"Captain's Island.

"Execution Rocks."

I keep going, naming and repeating and searching the horizon, till I make it to the spot where the harbor opens up and flows swiftly out to the Sound.

"David's.

"Neptune.

"Schultz's.

"Pine."

I cut the motor, thread the oars through the holders, and stroke on the starboard side only, making the *Angler* turn circles so I can take in the whole entire world.

20

JOY

THE POLICE HAD NO QUESTIONS FOR US. IT WAS MORE OF A
condolence call. The other nurses at the hospital where
my mother works knew Lukas and I were friends, and they
asked the officers to tell us in person.

I remember.

The sound of the wind pounding outside our windows
the rest of the morning.

The sound of crying. And that's when my silence began.

But it feels better to talk now. And to listen. I had no
idea how hurt and scared my parents were, not just by *my*
grief, but by their loss, too. They loved Lukas. Of course
they did.

So maybe I'll never know what Lukas wanted me to find
when I got back home, but maybe it's just *this*. Right here.
My family, my mom and dad, Natalia, Isabel and Davy, mac
'n' cheese, applesauce, peas, and cake.

Lukas did love cake.

Peas, not so much.

Maybe this is all he wanted me to find.

I have to be okay with that.

He'd like to know we are talking about him. I don't know how long we go around the room, sharing stories, trying to guess what Lukas might have meant by his last clue. I'm not worried about figuring it out; it just feels good to be talking about it.

About Lukas.

LUKAS

LIKE THE FONSECAS' APARTMENT BUILDING, THE SOUND WAY out here is dead quiet this early in the morning. Only me and a few scattered clamming boats. But they're still inland some, closer to shore. By noon, the water will be busy with sailboats and motorboats, and if they saw me out here by myself, surely someone would make me go home. But now it's just me and those few distant clammers, who have been up since before dawn and are happy enough to leave me alone.

I drop the oar, spread my arms, tilt my head back against the rubber edge of the *Angler* like a pillow, and close my eyes.

These are the people I need to think about: Mom, Justin, Rand, me, and Joy.

I start with Rand and Mom, because that's hard. I'll save Joy for later, because that's easy. The stuff about her, I've already decided.

Mom and Rand. A lump catches in my throat, but the water rocks the boat and I try to remember Rand in the beginning. Back when he was laughing all the time, and taking Mom out on dates, and giving us fist bumps and fake-out high fives. Back when the sides of his eyes would crinkle up like accordions, making him look older than he is, because of all the hard work he does outside for his construction job. Or because he's out riding his motorcycle. Or fishing on the water.

"I'm a victim of the elements," he once told Justin when Justin wouldn't believe he was only three years older than Mom.

And something else, the most important thing I remember: the look on his face when Mom made him promise.

"Don't come back, Rand. Not unless you've done the work. Gone to meetings. Stayed sober for at least six months."

And what he said back: "I promise you, Mel. I promise. Tell the boys I'm sorry. I promise."

I sit up in the *Angler*, my heart doing flips full of hope.

I'm sure that is why he's back! That he's done the work, and that Mom just didn't want to tell us unless she was sure.

But now she is. And so him being back is okay.

I lie back again and smile, amazed at how the sunshine that manages to break through the gathering clouds makes actual slanted rays of light, like you'd see in a painting, like a golden curtain that's shielding the shore.

The shore, and home, and Joy.

Five more minutes and I'll be ready to go back there.

21

JOY

THE STREETLAMPS ARE STARTING TO FLICKER ON OUTSIDE. Our windows are open because it's already cooler at night, and the crickets in the grass are singing their end-of-summer songs.

"What do you think?" I ask everyone. "What did he mean, he *planted* it for me? He planted *all* the clues for me."

"Read it again," my dad says.

I look down at the paper, creased with folds and time. "'When you get there, go slow, though you won't miss a clue, you may miss the best part I planted for you.'"

"Could something be hidden in the house?" Natalia asks.

It doesn't seem likely, since Lukas would never have been in our house when we weren't home.

"Maybe he was going to come over with a plant," my mother tries. "Like a real plant, or flowers."

That's a nice thought to linger on, but my dad abruptly stands up.

"What's the noise?" he asks. "Shh. Shh . . ."

When it is quiet, we all hear. Something like a whimpering.

Davy, who has been silent the whole time—but, of course, he always is—points to the corner of the room, where Isabel is curled up into a tiny little ball.

"Oh, I'm sorry." I run over and put my arms around her. "This must be so sad for you. We're sorry. We shouldn't be talking like this in front of you. Did we make you sad?"

But when she looks up at me, I know *that's* not what's wrong. It's something else. Davy is right beside her.

He uses his words so sparingly, but now he's determined. "Tell them, Izzie," he says.

I want to shake her and say, "What have you done now, Isabel?" But one look from Davy tells me not to. So I wait. We all just wait, for what feels like a very long time.

Isabel talks so softly. "I had to hide, you know, like I always used to, in my hiding place. I was so scared. The police and everyone crying. And I just found it. The box, the red box, it was there in the plant, and, I don't know, I thought that's why the police came. I thought that's why you were so upset, Jolie. I thought you were in trouble or something. I didn't know. I just wanted to help you. I thought if I got rid of it, the police would go away."

She's crying now.

No one says anything.

Our mother gets down on the floor next to Isabel. "No

183

one is mad at you, Izzie. No matter what. But you can tell us. Whatever you know. You should tell us now."

"I thought if I got rid of it, everything would be better," Isabel says. "I just wanted everyone to stop crying. I was scared. And then I just never thought about it again. I forgot. I forgot until now, the plant. It was in the plant outside our door. Do you forgive me, Joy?"

"Of course, I do, Izzie. Look, it was a horrible morning. No one knew what to do. It's okay." But it takes everything I have not to shake her memory right out of her little head.

Our mother is talking slowly. "Do you remember what you did with it?"

Isabel nods.

We all wait.

And my blood is pounding again, but this time I have my family with me. Each one of them is absorbing the racing thumps in my chest, catching them before my whole heart falls on the ground.

We all wait.

"I buried it," Isabel says. "Outside. In the courtyard."

LUKAS

AND THEN I'M FLOATING AND DRIFTING AND SMILING AND breathing, because I know how everything is going to be okay.

Justin is going to graduate. And Rand is better, and back for good this time.

And today is Joy's birthday, and she'll be so happy when she sees the work I did to make it good for her.

I think about each clue I wrote, from Vincent's to Thea's to B&B's. To the library and to Mr. Carter's amazing secret tree, and the clue that will lead her back home again.

To the red box I left outside her door.

To the heart necklace.

And the note I wrote for her.

But the tree. The tree is the best part.

I close my eyes and let the tree float in, its branches like arms spreading wide, taking up all the worried space in my head. And I imagine how Joy will feel when she figures it out and finds the clue, and when I tell her the story of Mr. Carter and his wife. And it hits me now, as I picture her standing there like that, listening to me, talking to me, that I already know the truth. I know what she said on the phone last night. It's not stupid or unthinkable or wrong.

"I love you," she said. "I love you."

I can hear her words clear as day.

And I can feel me and Joy, together, in the shade of that summer tree. As if it's only my imagination letting in those cool August shadows, and not a storm moving in and the waves kicking up, and a jagged streak lighting up the swiftly darkening sky.

22

JOY

THE SUN IS SETTING BY THE TIME WE ALL GET OUTSIDE. IT PAINTS a beautiful picture of colors across the horizon, and it reminds me of a poem that I had to memorize in sixth-grade English.

I picked one of the shortest ones I could find from the list of approved poets. No more Jack Prelutsky or Shel Silverstein. We were in middle school now. I picked Emily Dickinson.

> *Nature rarer uses yellow*
> *Than another hue;*
> *Saves she all of that for sunsets,—*
> *Prodigal of blue,*
>
> *Spending scarlet like a woman,*
> *Yellow she affords*
> *Only scantly and selectly,*
> *Like a lover's words.*

I had no idea what *prodigal* meant; I still don't. But I remember how embarrassed I was when I finally had to say those last words out loud in class, in front of everyone, even though I knew how beautiful they were.

Maybe because the words made me think about Lukas.

"Do you remember where you buried it?" my dad is asking Isabel.

No one is saying anything, as if just our talking might scare the memory right out of her brain. We are standing around the little patch of grass outside, in the center of our complex, and it doesn't look so huge at all anymore. It just looks like a square of grass, where two little kids thought they could plant a candy garden. When the world was much smaller, and so much easier.

"Here?" Isabel points.

My dad has a small gardening shovel, and he pokes around. "Hmm, are you sure?"

Isabel is trying hard. I know she is. Even if there is something under the dirt, it's been a whole year of rain and snow and seeding and mowing, more rain and more snow. She couldn't have buried a box very deep. For all we know, it got raked up with the leaves and thrown away as garbage.

"Maybe there?" She points to another spot, and then another. Each time, our dad stabs the dirt carefully and stands up again, shaking his head.

"Hey, what are you all doing here? You can't do that," Mr. Sweeny shouts.

Our dad steps over the little metal fencing and reaches out his hand. "Mr. Fonseca. Building two, apartment twelve."

"I know who you are. But that doesn't explain why you are digging up the lawn."

So my dad explains about that day and about the box, and as soon as he mentions Lukas, the expression on Mr. Sweeny's angry face changes. It always does.

"Terrible tragedy," he says. "I liked that kid a lot." Then he looks at me. "You're looking for a box?" he says. "A red box?"

"Yes!" I say. "How did you know?" But Mr. Sweeny is already walking away.

He turns around. "Well, c'mon. Follow me. Does anyone ever bother checking the lost-and-found?"

"Of course," you are saying. *"Where else do you look for something you lost?"*

Are you laughing? I hope you are laughing.

Mr. Sweeny takes a lot of pride in keeping the grounds around our buildings clean. It turns out he saw a red box poking out of the dirt that very morning. That very day.

How could he forget that day?

He didn't know who it belonged to—any name that might have been there had rubbed off in the dirt—so he brought it back to his office. He keeps a shelf in here, he tells us, for everything he picks up around the complex: tons of sunglasses, a single sneaker, flip-flops—lots of flip-flops—T-shirts, towels, water bottles, hairbrushes, a fork. If it's a book or a letter, he's not going to look through it or open it. He keeps it all in the lost-and-found, and after one year, he tosses it all out.

"It's none of my business," he says.

Mr. Sweeny reaches to the top shelf, takes down a small red cardboard box, and hands it to me.

And now I am holding it in my hands.

23

JOY

THIS MORNING FEELS LIKE SO, SO LONG AGO, AND A YEAR feels like yesterday.

There is my new guitar, just propped up against my bed. There is my bed, the Ariana Grande easy-chord songbook on top. There is my desk, the bottom drawer left partially open. I was in such a rush this morning.

I think I'm going to text Audrey and see if she wants to come over and "play." She has a really great voice.

My family left me alone when I asked them to, but I can hear Isabel and Davy right outside my door. Davy is kicking the wall, and Isabel is whisper-shouting for him to stop. We are going to have dinner soon, and then cake.

Aunt Idalia and Uncle Joey will come over, our cousins Aiden and Zoey and Holden. The house will be a zoo. I would always warn him, but I know Lukas loved it. He let my little cousins climb all over him, too. He ate seconds and thirds of mac 'n' cheese when my mom offered. He stayed for candles and dessert and more presents.

But this year he's not here.

Only this red box.

Slowly I take off the paper, carefully, like even the wrapper is a gift I almost didn't find. I open it, and there is a letter, folded tightly. And when I take out the letter, there is something underneath. A sparkling gold chain, with a delicate red heart dangling between my fingers.

Isabel and Davy are beside themselves outside my door, I can just feel it. And hear it. The kicking is louder; whispering isn't even attempted anymore.

But I need more time.

I need more rainbow cupcakes and another candy garden. I wonder if things will get better or get worse, but I imagine it's probably a little of both. It's probably about realizing that you don't get everything you want, sometimes not even close.

I unclasp the chain, reach around under my hair, and I lock the ends together. I can feel the heart pendant resting right in that little dip in the center of my throat.

I don't want to ever take it off.

This is part of what it is to be thirteen.

To go on a journey and end up right back home. To love someone who loved you back, and still have to say goodbye to them.

"I'll be right there!" I shout toward my bedroom door.

I know Isabel is so happy we found the box.

I reach up and touch the necklace, the heart around my

neck. I wonder what this year would have been like if Lukas hadn't died.

Would he be here with me, today?

Would I have put on this necklace and never taken it off?

But one thing I know for sure, we'd always have been friends. We would always know parts of each other that no one else knew. Keepers of Secrets, Wizards of Clues, Growers of Gardens, King and Queen of Summer Birthdays, Holders of Hearts.

The letter is pressed into such a tiny square, it is hard to unfold. It opens up once, twice. Three, four, five times before it is fully flat and I can read it. My throat isn't constricting or stinging; it just hurts, but I can take it.

Dear Joy,
    Justin says I'm a jerk for doing this.
    But then he thinks our hunts are stupid, too. ☺
    Maybe he's right, but I think he just doesn't understand what it means to have a good friend, someone you like to be with more than anyone else. Someone who makes the crappiest days better, and the bad stuff funny, and awful summer birthdays the best. Someone you care more about than anyone.

Someone you love.

This is for you.

P.S. Happy birthday every birthday,
always,

Lukas

ACKNOWLEDGMENTS

Gae and Nora warmly thank:

Jim McCarthy and Katelyn Detweiler, our skilled, calming, and accessible literary agents, who worked so lovingly in concert to find a perfect home for this book.

Karen Greenberg, our editor, who fell in love with Joy and Lukas just as we did, and helped bring them so beautifully and fully to life.

Esther Lin, Artie Bennett, Alison Kolani, Amy Schroeder, and Diane João, meticulous and artistic copy editors.

April Ward for our amazing and beautiful cover design, and Ken Crossland because the inside counts just as much.

Behind the scenes: production manager Jonathan Morris, and managing editor Jake Eldred.

It really does take a village.

To the whole team at Knopf/Penguin Random House, our appreciation is boundless.

And with gratitude and love: Ginger Polisner, Lesley Burnap, Sidney Snyder, and Melissa Guerrette for their fast and enthusiastic early reads; LuAnn O'Hair, an exceptional educator, and her astute 2018–19 eighth-grade class at Forgan Public School in Oklahoma, who read an early draft of "Finding Joy" and encouraged us with their excitement for Joy and Lukas's story; Cindy Beth Minnich for her constant support of us and our stories (and of writers everywhere); and the extraordinary Leslie Connor, Tony Abbott, and Wendy Mass for letting us put their heartfelt praise on the cover.

And, mostly, and always, to our families, for their unwavering belief in us.

Carol Carrick

·Valentine·

Illustrated by Paddy Bouma

Clarion Books ◆ New York

Clarion Books
a Houghton Mifflin Company imprint
215 Park Avenue South, New York, NY 10003
Text copyright © 1995 by Carol Carrick
Illustrations copyright © 1995 by Paddy Bouma

The illustrations for this book were executed in watercolor
on Fabriano cold press watercolor paper.
The text was set in 14/18 point Garamond.

Printed in the USA.

Library of Congress Cataloging-in-Publication Data

Carrick, Carol.
        Valentine / by Carol Carrick ; illustrated by Paddy Bouma.
            p.   cm.
        Summary: While waiting for her mother to come home
from work on Valentine's Day, Heather helps her grandmother rescue
a newborn lamb and bake a special cooky.
        ISBN 0-395-66554-X
        [1. Sheep—Fiction. 2. Valentine's Day—Fiction. 3.
Grandmothers—Fiction. 4. Mothers and daughters—Fiction]
I. Bouma, Paddy, ill. II. Title.
PZ7.C2344Val   1995
[E]—dc20   94-35911
                                                                              CIP
                                                                              AC

        WOZ   10 9 8 7 6 5 4 3 2

For Heather and Noemi
—*C.C.*

For Elizabeth
—*P.B.*

It was still dark when Mama put on her coat and hugged Heather good-bye. Mama worked in an office.

Heather held on extra tight to her mother. "Don't go," she said. "It's Valentine's Day."

Mama gave her a kiss. "It's still a work day for me," she said.

"Why do you always have to go to work?" said Heather. "I don't want you to go."

"I'm sorry," said Mama. "I would rather stay home with you."

Heather and Mama were living with Grandma. Heather felt sad as she watched Mama drive down the road. It would be dark again before her mother came home. She held her blanket against her face. It smelled like oatmeal and like Mama.

3

"Such a sad face on this special day!" said Grandma. "Help me make cookie valentines."

Grandma mixed butter and sugar. She added flour to make a soft dough. It felt like the clay Heather played with when she went to day care.

Grandma let Heather roll out the dough. When it was flat, they cut out cookies that looked just like Grandma's animals—chickens, cats, and sheep. Then they cut out a heart cookie for Mama's valentine.

"Can we eat one now?" asked Heather.

"No," said Grandma. "They have to bake first."

Heather sighed. She always had to wait. Wait for Valentine's Day. Wait for cookies to bake. Wait for Mama to come home.

Grandma put the first two pans in the oven. "Now! Shall we make a quick check to see how Clover is doing?" Clover was Grandma's favorite sheep.

Grandma went out to the pen where the sheep was waiting to have her lambs. Heather followed slowly, dragging her blanket.

"Heather, come here!" Grandma sounded excited. "Clover had her babies. Two of them!" Already, the newborn lambs were on their feet and getting milk from their mother.

Heather peeked in at them. "Grandma, look! There's one more."
Behind Clover lay another little lamb. Heather reached through
the fencing to touch him. He felt stiff and cold. And he didn't
move. Something was very wrong.

"Poor little thing," said Grandma.

Heather clutched her blanket. "Is he dead?" she asked in a small voice.

Grandma picked up the lamb. She held him next to her cheek, the way Heather was holding her blanket. "I think I can feel his breath," she said. "Let's take him inside where it's warm."

Grandma filled the kitchen sink with water and put the lamb in the warm bath. She held his head up so he could breathe.

"Are you washing him because he's dirty?" asked Heather.

"No, dear, I'm trying to get him warm. Bring me a towel from the bathroom."

Heather hurried to get him her own towel.

Grandma lifted the lamb from the sink and wrapped him in the towel, but he still didn't move.

"Grandma! The cookies! I can smell them," said Heather.

"Heavens!" said Grandma. "I forgot. Good thing I have you to help me." She handed the lamb to Heather.

"Here," Grandma said. "Sit with the lamb by the stove while I rescue the cookies. I hope they haven't burned."

Grandma took out the pans. Heather could see that the cookies were too brown around the edges.

"I think they're tastier that way," said Grandma, but Heather
didn't care about cookies now. She looked at the little lamb in
her arms. His eyes were still closed and he didn't move.

"Grandma, I don't want the lamb to die," Heather said, and she
began to cry.

Grandmother opened up the towel. The lamb's wet hair stuck to his wrinkled skin. Grandmother put her hand behind the lamb's front leg. She took Heather's hand and laid it on the same place. Heather could feel his heartbeat, just barely.

Grandma brought Mama's hair dryer from the bathroom and rubbed the lamb dry in the warm air.

The lamb made the smallest little sound and his head moved.

Heather smiled.

"Can you hold him," Grandma said, "while I fix him some milk?"

Heather cradled the little lamb in her lap. "There, there," she said, patting him the way Mama patted Heather when she was hurt. "There, there." Then she covered him with her blanket. The blanket always made *her* feel better.

Grandma filled one of Heather's old baby bottles with warm milk. She pushed the nipple into the lamb's mouth. His lips moved. He began sucking noisily, pulling at the bottle with his mouth. Under Heather's blanket, the lamb's tail wagged. That made Heather laugh.

When the milk was gone, the lamb lifted its head and made a bleating sound, "M-a-a m-a-a-a." He began to struggle.

"He's looking for his mother," said Grandma.

"Will you put him back in the barn?" asked Heather. She didn't want him to go.

"Not today," said Grandmother. "We'll have to go on feeding him with a bottle. His mother has two other lambs to feed, and she's doing the best she can."

Heather was glad. "There, there, lamb," she said. "I'll take care of you."

Soon the lamb was asleep in the laundry basket.

23

Grandma put the rest of the cookies in the oven. One of them was the heart-shaped cookie for Mama.

When Mama came home, Heather showed her the lamb. That was when she knew what to call him. "His name is Valentine," she told Mama.

"He needs me," Heather said proudly. "His mother can't take care of him."

Then Heather showed Mama the cookie cats, and the chickens, and the little sheep that looked like Grandma's.

"I made this heart for you," said Heather, "because I love you."

"And I love you, too," said Mama.

"M-a-a," called Valentine, lifting his head.